52

LONGMANS' ABRIDGED BOOKS

A TALE OF TWO CITIES

Longmans' Abridged Books

A TALE OF TWO CITIES

WUTHERING HEIGHTS

PRIDE AND PREJUDICE

LITTLE WOMEN

A Tale of Two Cities

CHARLES DICKENS

ABRIDGEMENT AND INTRODUCTION BY
D. K. SWAN, M.A.

LONGMANS

LONGMANS, GREEN AND CO LTD
6 & 7 CLIFFORD STREET, LONDON W 1

THIBAULT HOUSE, THIBAULT SQUARE, CAPE TOWN
602–611 LONSDALE STREET, MELBOURNE C 1
443 LOCKHART ROAD, HONG KONG
ACCRA, AUCKLAND, IBADAN
KINGSTON (JAMAICA), KUALA LUMPUR
LAHORE, NAIROBI, SALISBURY (RHODESIA)

LONGMANS, GREEN AND CO INC
119 WEST 40TH STREET, NEW YORK 18

LONGMANS, GREEN AND CO
20 CRANFIELD ROAD, TORONTO 16

ORIENT LONGMANS PRIVATE LTD
CALCUTTA, BOMBAY, MADRAS
DELHI, HYDERABAD, DACCA

First published in this series 1959

PRINTED IN GREAT BRITAIN BY RICHARD CLAY AND COMPANY LTD
BUNGAY, SUFFOLK

CONTENTS

THE LIFE OF CHARLES DICKENS

CHARLES DICKENS was born at Portsmouth in 1812. His father, a naval clerk, was several times transferred, so that Charles's boyhood was not spent in one place. Probably he was happiest at Chatham, where his family went when he was four, and where he went to school. When he was nine his family moved to London, and life became very hard. Instead of going to school, Charles had to look after five brothers and sisters. When he was twelve he had to go to work in a boot-blacking factory while his father was in a debtors' prison. In those days a debtor could be imprisoned until his debts were paid. Fortunately for Charles's father, a relative left him some money. On his release he sent Charles to a small school where he received education of a sort for less than two years, leaving just after his fourteenth birthday to become a boy clerk in a lawyer's office.

So far as school education was concerned, it was a very poor start for one of the world's best-known writers, but Charles Dickens had great gifts which helped him to make good use of these early troubles. In the ups and downs of those years he was thrown among all sorts of people. He had wonderful powers of observation and a great understanding of human nature, which later he was able to put down on paper, so that many of the people he met at that time came to life again in the books he wrote.

While he worked in the lawyer's office he watched those who came and went, and again stored away the results of his observation of courts, lawyers, witnesses and others. These results, too, you will find in his books, especially in *A Tale of Two Cities*. At the same time he was studying shorthand and was reading every obtainable book which would help him towards a better career. He wanted to be a writer, and in particular to be a newspaper reporter of political speeches and the debates in Parliament, so he threw all his tremendous energy and determination into preparing himself for such work by making up for the slightness of his education and increasing his store of general knowledge.

At the age of nineteen Charles Dickens achieved his first ambition. He became a reporter for the *Morning Chronicle* and other papers, spending much time in the reporters' gallery in the House of Commons but also making many journeys throughout England by stage-coach and post-chaise to report speeches by leading politicians. He was soon recognized as the ablest reporter of the time. He was still observing acutely everything that went on around him and storing away exact mind pictures of how the people he met looked and spoke and acted. He began to write short stories or 'sketches' into which he put some of the portraits stored in his mind.

Dickens' sketches became popular, and it was because of this that he was asked to write the stories to go with a series of drawings by the comic artist, Seymour. These joyful stories of *Pickwick* appeared in monthly instalments, and before long had attracted very large numbers of readers. From that time (1836) onwards he wrote a succession of novels, most of which are still favourites today; *The Adventures of Oliver Twist*, *Nicholas Nickleby*, *The Old Curiosity Shop*, *Barnaby Rudge* and *David Copperfield* are some of those which were written before *A Tale of Two Cities* (1859). Nearly all of them appeared in what we should now call serial form. They were filled with the characters Dickens knew so well how to create, and his ever-growing reading public looked forward with excitement to each month's instalment. It was a sentimental age; it is said that when poor Little Nell died in the story of *The Old Curiosity Shop* there were floods of tears shed on both sides of the Atlantic.

Dickens himself became so well loved that when he died in 1870 many thousands of people went into mourning for him. His grave and memorial are in Westminster Abbey among those of the great and famous men of British history.

A SUMMARY OF THE PLOT

MR. LORRY and Lucie Manette go from London to Paris where Lucie's father, Doctor Manette, is at Defarge's wine-shop suffering from loss of memory after release from long imprisonment in the Bastille. Back in London, where Doctor Manette is recovering, Mr. Lorry and Lucie are witnesses at the trial for treason of Charles Darnay. Darnay is acquitted, largely through the quick intelligence of Sydney Carton, whose features are remarkably like Darnay's. Really a French marquis, Darnay works for his living in England because he hates the oppression of the people by the nobility of France. So great is this oppression that the French, led by such people as Defarge and his wife, are preparing to rebel. In London Charles Darnay falls in love with Lucie. They are married after Charles has told Doctor Manette that he is really the Marquis St. Evrémonde, promising, on the Doctor's insistence, to tell nobody else. Sydney Carton, too, loves Lucie, but knows himself unworthy of her. He promises, however, that if ever it is necessary, he will give his life for 'a life you love'. The revolution breaks out in France, Defarge distinguishing himself at the attack on the Bastille. Our characters are drawn to Paris, first Mr. Lorry then Charles, who goes to save a family servant. When Charles is imprisoned as an aristocrat, the Doctor and Lucie follow. The Doctor secures Charles's release, but he has to face a second trial at which there is read a document found by Defarge in the Bastille in which the Doctor had told of his imprisonment resulting from the enmity of Charles's uncle, the former marquis. He is condemned to death, but Sydney Carton keeps his promise to Lucie by saving Charles at the cost of his own life. Relying on the similarity of their features, he takes Charles's place among the condemned. Mr. Lorry brings the Doctor, Lucie and Charles to safety in England while Sydney goes bravely to the guillotine, comforting a little seamstress who is to die with him.

COMMENTS ON THE CHARACTERS

THE notes which follow may help you to arrange your ideas of the main characters in *A Tale of Two Cities*. They are given in the order in which the characters appear in the story. The numbers in brackets give the pages on which there is something to support what is said, but you may find other passages which give you further ideas or even suggest a different view of some of the characters.

Mr. Jarvis Lorry has worked for many years for Tellson's Bank and thinks of himself as a mere business machine. In fact, he frequently uses the word 'business' (7–8, 15, 16, 21, 87), but there is a very human look in his eye (4), and he is really a very tender-hearted old bachelor (52, 87). He says he is timorous (32), but in time of trouble he is a very brave and capable friend (89, 187–8). Such kindly old gentlemen appear in a number of Dickens's books.

Lucie Manette is beautiful (6, 67, 92), but it is not colourless prettiness. Her way of knitting her brow (6, 91) shows that there are depths in her character. In spite of her real femininity (48), she has great courage and devotion to duty (129, 166). We are struck most of all by her sympathy and understanding (20, 72–3) and her insight into the true character of Sydney Carton.

Miss Pross is physically strong (9) and pretends to be hard (49, 50) and without imagination (50). She is the devoted protector of Lucie (9, 49), and the great courage this devotion gives her enables her to play an important part in covering the final escape (191–6).

Ernest Defarge, sometimes called Jacques, the keeper of a wine-shop in Paris, is an example of the type of men who became leaders of the French Revolution (95–7). He looks good-humoured but implacable (11), a dangerous man (14). As a young man he has been Doctor Manette's servant (14, 165) and has feelings which would keep him from heartless cruelty if he were not completely dominated by his wife (56, 85, 114, 173, 188–9).

Madame Defarge, his wife, is hard, pitiless and bitter (57, 96, 123, 189). She makes no mistakes (12) until the end, is quick-witted and cunning (12, 79, 80–4), and inspires fear in those who meet her (125, 143, 189). She shows humanity only in her support of her husband.

Doctor Manette has suffered greatly in mind and body as a result of his imprisonment (16–23, 87–9), but makes a remarkable recovery under Lucie's devoted care (47). He is a good father (88), fair-minded (69) and of great courage (88, 120) and capability (126–8, 135–7), but never quite free from the danger of a relapse (51, 70, 89, 175).

Charles Darnay has a manly, quiet courage (26). He is gentle and kind (33). An idealist, he is well aware of many of the wrongs done by his family (63–4) and is ready to seek work in a foreign land rather than claim his inheritance and be in any way dependent on a system which gives wealth to the few at the expense of the many (64–5, 66–7). His courage is further shown by his willingness to risk known (104) danger in going to France (109) and by the manner in which he bears his misfortunes (167, 180). We know that he would never have let Sydney Carton take his place if he had been conscious (183).

Sydney Carton is the most complex character in the book. Apart from a remarkable similarity in looks (36, 172), he seems to have nothing in common with Charles Darnay. He appears careless, slovenly, idle and reckless (26, 36, 37, 39, 44), and it is certain that when we first meet him he drinks too much (40, 41, 43, 142). We notice, though, that he seems to have quick powers of observation (36, 37) and understanding (38). It is a good sign that he is dissatisfied with himself (43, 71, 147). We discover that he is capable of great mental effort (45–6), though he is moody, now up, now down, and given to fits of despondency (46–7, 71). It is possible, we think, that his failings may be due in some way to the early loss of his parents (149–50). He covers up his good nature (41), but, though he would not believe it of himself, we begin to see, with Lucie, that he is 'capable of good things, gentle things, even magnanimous things' (92). As his character develops under her good influence, we see that he is capable of deep devotion and sincerity (71–4, 146, 169), and we are glad when, having given up strong drink (144, 171), he puts his great mental powers to good use (172–4), and then, as he makes his great sacrifice to save another, is able to be of even further service, so that the little seamstress says (199) 'I think you were sent to me by Heaven.'

1 · THE DOVER MAIL

It was the best of times, it was the worst of times, it was the age of wisdom, it was the age of foolishness, it was the epoch of belief, it was the epoch of incredulity, it was the season of Light, it was the season of Darkness, it was the spring of hope, it was the winter of despair, we had everything before us, we were all going direct to Heaven, we were all going direct the other way. There were a king with a large jaw and a queen with a plain face, on the throne of England; there were a king with a large jaw and a queen with a fair face, on the throne of France. It was the year of Our Lord one thousand seven hundred and seventy-five.

It was the Dover road that lay, on a Friday night late in November, before the first of the persons with whom this history has business. The Dover road lay before the Dover mail, as it lumbered up Shooter's Hill. He walked uphill in the mire by the side of the mail, as the rest of the passengers did; not because they had the least relish for walking exercise, under the circumstances, but because the hill, and the harness, and the mud, and the mail, were all so heavy, that the horses had three times already come to a stop, besides once drawing the coach across the road.

There was a steaming mist in all the hollows. It was dense enough to shut out everything from the light of the coach-lamps but a few yards of road.

Two other passengers, besides the one, were plodding up the hill by the side of the mail. All three were wrapped to the cheek-bones and over the ears, and wore jack-boots. Not one of the three could have said, from anything he saw, what either of the other two was like; and each was hidden under many wrappers from the eyes of his two companions. In those days, travellers were very shy of being confidential, for anybody on the road might be a robber or in league with robbers.

'Wo-ho!' said the coachman. 'So, then! One more pull and you're at the top and be damned to you, for I have had trouble enough to get you to it!—Joe!'

'What do you say, Tom?'

They both listened.

'I say a horse at a canter coming up, Joe.'

'I say a horse at a gallop, Tom,' returned the guard. 'Gentlemen! In the king's name, all of you!'

With this hurried adjuration, he cocked his blunderbuss, and stood on the offensive.

The stillness consequent on the cessation of the rumbling and labouring of the coach, added to the stillness of the night, made it very quiet indeed. The sound of a horse at a gallop came fast and furiously up the hill.

'So-ho!' the guard sang out, as loud as he could roar. 'Ho there! Stand! I shall fire!'

The pace was suddenly checked, and, with much splashing and floundering, a man's voice called from the mist, 'Is that the Dover mail?'

'Why do you want to know?'

'I want a passenger if it is. Mr. Jarvis Lorry.'

'Keep where you are,' the guard called to the voice in the mist, 'because, if I should make a mistake, it could never be set right in your lifetime. Gentleman of the name of Lorry, answer straight.'

'What is the matter?' asked the passenger, then, 'Who wants me? Is it Jerry?'

'Yes, Mr. Lorry.'

'What is the matter?'

'A despatch sent to you from T. and Co.'

'I know this messenger, guard,' said Mr. Lorry. 'He may come close; there's nothing wrong.'

'I hope there ain't, but I can't make so sure of that,' said the guard. 'Hallo you! Come on at a footpace. And if you've got holsters to that saddle, don't let me see your hand go near them.'

The figures of a horse and rider came slowly through the eddying mist. The rider stooped and handed the passenger a small folded paper. The rider's horse was blown, and both horse and rider were covered with mud, from the hoofs of the horse to the hat of the man.

'Guard!' said the passenger, in a tone of quiet business confidence.

The watchful guard, with his right hand at the stock of his raised blunderbuss, his left at the barrel, and his eye on the horseman, answered curtly, 'Sir.'

'There is nothing to fear. I belong to Tellson's Bank. I am going to Paris on business. I may read this?'

'If so be as you're quick, sir.'

He opened it in the light of the coach-lamp on that side, and read—first to himself and then aloud: ' "Wait at Dover for Mam'selle." It's not long, you see, guard. Jerry, say that my answer was, RECALLED TO LIFE.'

Jerry started in his saddle. 'That's a blazing strange answer, too,' said he.

'Take that message back, and they will know that I received this, as well as if I wrote. Make the best of your way. Good night.'

The coach lumbered on again, with heavier wreaths of mist closing round it as it began the descent.

When the mail got successfully to Dover, in the course of the forenoon, the head drawer at the Royal George Hotel opened the coach-door as his custom was. He did it with some flourish of ceremony, for a mail journey from London in winter was an achievement to congratulate an adventurous traveller upon.

By that time, there was only one adventurous traveller left to be congratulated; for the two others had been set down at their respective roadside destinations.

'There will be a packet-boat to Calais, to-morrow, drawer?'

'Yes, sir, if the weather holds and the wind sets tolerable fair. The tide will serve pretty nicely at about two in the afternoon, sir. Bed, sir?'

'I shall not go to bed till night; but I want a bedroom, and a barber.'

'And then breakfast sir? Yes sir. That way, sir if you please. Show Concord! Gentleman's valise and hot water to Concord.'

Some time later Mr. Lorry, a gentleman of sixty, formally dressed in a brown suit of clothes, pretty well worn, but very well kept, with large square cuffs and large flaps to the pockets, left Concord on his way to breakfast.

The coffee-room had no other occupant, that forenoon, than the gentleman in brown. His breakfast-table was drawn before the fire, and as he sat, with its light shining on him, waiting for the meal, he sat so still, that he might have been sitting for his portrait.

A face habitually suppressed and quieted, was still lighted up by a pair of moist bright eyes that it must have cost their owner, in years gone by, some pains to drill to the composed and reserved expression of Tellson's Bank.

Completing his resemblance to a man who was sitting for

his portrait, Mr. Lorry dropped off to sleep. The arrival of his breakfast roused him, and he said to the drawer, as he moved his chair to it:

'I wish accommodation prepared for a young lady who may come here at any time to-day. She may ask for Mr. Jarvis Lorry, or she may only ask for a gentleman from Tellson's Bank. Please to let me know.'

'Yes, sir. Tellson's Bank in London, sir?'

'Yes.'

'Yes, sir. We have oftentimes the honour to entertain your gentlemen in their travelling backwards and forwards betwixt London and Paris, sir. A vast deal of travelling, sir, in Tellson and Company's House.'

'Yes. We are quite a French House, as well as an English one.'

'Yes, sir. Not much in the habit of such travelling yourself, I think, sir?'

'Not of late years. It is fifteen years since we—since I—came last from France.'

When Mr. Lorry had finished his breakfast, he went out for a stroll on the beach.

As the day declined into the afternoon, and the air, which had been at intervals clear enough to allow the French coast to be seen, became again charged with mist and vapour, Mr. Lorry's thoughts seemed to cloud too. When it was dark, he sat before the coffee-room fire, awaiting his dinner as he had awaited his breakfast.

After dinner he had just poured out his last glassful of wine, when a rattling of wheels came up the narrow street, and rumbled into the inn-yard.

He set down his glass untouched. 'This is Mam'selle!' said he.

In a very few minutes the waiter came in to announce that Miss Manette had arrived from London. Miss Manette was extremely anxious to see the gentleman from Tellson's immediately, if it suited his pleasure and convenience. The gentleman from Tellson's had nothing left for it but to empty his glass and follow the waiter to Miss Manette's apartment.

Standing to receive him was a young lady of not more than seventeen, in a riding-cloak, and still holding her straw travelling-hat by its ribbon in her hand. As his eyes rested on a short, slight, pretty figure, a quantity of golden hair, a pair of blue eyes that met his own with an inquiring look, and a forehead with a singular capacity (remembering how young and smooth it was) of lifting and knitting itself into an expression that was not quite one of perplexity, or wonder, or alarm, or merely of a bright fixed attention, though it included all the four expressions—as his eyes rested on these things, a sudden vivid likeness passed before him, of a child whom he had held in his arms on the passage across that very Channel, one cold time, when the hail drifted heavily and the sea ran high. The likeness passed away, and he made his formal bow to Miss Manette.

'Pray take a seat, sir,' she said, in a very clear and pleasant young voice. 'I received a letter from the Bank, sir, yesterday, informing me that some—discovery—respecting the small property of my father, whom I never saw—so long dead—rendered it necessary that I should go to Paris, there to communicate with a gentleman of the Bank despatched to Paris for the purpose. I replied to the Bank, sir, that I should esteem it highly if I might be permitted to place myself, during the journey, under that worthy gentleman's protection. The gentleman had left London, but I think a mes-

senger was sent after him to beg the favour of his waiting for me here.'

'I was happy,' said Mr. Lorry, 'to be entrusted with the charge. I shall be more happy to execute it.'

'Sir, I thank you indeed. It was told me by the Bank that the gentleman would explain to me the details of the business, and that I must prepare myself to find them of a surprising nature. I naturally have a strong and eager interest to know what they are.'

'Naturally,' said Mr. Lorry. 'Yes—I——'

After a pause, he added:

'It is very difficult to begin.'

He did not begin, but, in his indecision, met her glance. The young forehead lifted itself into that singular expression —but it was pretty and characteristic, besides being singular —and she raised her hand, as if she caught at some passing shadow.

'Are you quite a stranger to me, sir?'

'Miss Manette, I am a man of business. I have a business charge to acquit myself of. In your reception of it, don't heed me any more than if I were a speaking machine—truly, I am not much else. I will, with your leave, relate to you, miss, the story of one of our customers. He was a French gentleman; a scientific gentleman; a man of great acquirements—a Doctor.'

'Of Beauvais?'

'Why, yes, of Beauvais. Like Monsieur Manette, your father, the gentleman was of Beauvais. Like Monsieur Manette, your father, the gentleman was of repute in Paris. I had the honour of knowing him there. Our relations were business relations, but confidential. I was at that time in our French House, and had been—oh! twenty years.'

' "At that time"—I may ask, at what time, sir?'

'I speak, miss, of twenty years ago. He married—an English lady—and I was one of the trustees. His affairs, like the affairs of many other French gentlemen and French families, were entirely in Tellson's hands. In a similar way, I am, or I have been, trustee of one kind or other for scores of our customers. These are mere business relations, miss——'

'But this is my father's story, sir; and I begin to think'—the curiously roughened forehead was very intent upon him—'that when I was left an orphan through my mother's surviving my father only two years, it was you who brought me to England. I am almost sure it was you.'

Mr. Lorry took the hesitating little hand that confidingly advanced to take his.

'Miss Manette, it *was* I.'

Mr. Lorry went on to tell her, with much hesitation and insistence upon 'business', that her father had not died. He had suddenly and mysteriously disappeared. His wife feared that some enemy might have had him consigned to prison by obtaining a *lettre de cachet*, an infamous privilege exercised by the French nobility of that time, but, try as she might, she could learn nothing of his fate.

'When she died—I believe broken-hearted—having never slackened her unavailing search for your father, she left you, at two years old, to grow to be blooming, beautiful, and happy, without the dark cloud upon you of living in uncertainty whether your father soon wore his heart out in prison, or wasted there through many lingering years.'

The expression in the forehead, which had so particularly attracted his notice, had deepened into one of pain and horror.

'But he has been—been found. He is alive. Greatly changed, it is too probable; almost a wreck, it is possible; though we will hope the best. Still, alive. Your father has been taken to the house of an old servant in Paris, and we are going there: I, to identify him if I can: you, to restore him to life, love, duty, rest, comfort.'

A shiver ran through her frame. She said, in a low, distinct, awe-stricken voice, as if she were saying it in a dream:

'I am going to see his Ghost! It will be his Ghost—not him!'

A wild-looking woman, whom even in his agitation, Mr. Lorry observed to be all of a red colour, and to have red hair, and to be dressed in some extraordinary fashion, came into the room at that moment, took one look at Miss Manette, set a brawny hand upon Mr. Lorry's chest, and sent him flying back against the nearest wall.

('I really think this must be a man!' was Mr. Lorry's breathless reflection.)

'You in brown!' she said, indignantly, 'couldn't you tell her what you had to tell her, without frightening her to death?'

Mr. Lorry found the question so hard to answer, that he could only say:

'I hope she does well now.'

'No thanks to you in brown, if she does. My darling pretty!'

'I hope,' said Mr. Lorry, 'that you accompany Miss Manette to France?'

'A likely thing, too!' replied the strong woman. 'If it was ever intended that I should go across salt water, do you suppose Providence would have cast my lot in an island?'

2 · THE WINE-SHOP

A LARGE cask of wine had been dropped and broken, in the street. The accident had happened in getting it out of a cart; the cask had tumbled out with a run, the hoops had burst, and it lay on the stones just outside the door of the wine-shop, shattered like a walnut-shell.

All the people within reach had suspended their business, or their idleness, to run to the spot and drink the wine. The rough, irregular stones of the street, pointing every way, had dammed it into little pools; these were surrounded, each by its own jostling group or crowd.

A shrill sound of laughter and of amused voices—voices of men, women, and children—resounded in the street while this wine game lasted. The wine was red wine, and had stained the ground of the narrow street in the suburb of Saint Antoine, in Paris, where it was spilled. It had stained many hands, too, and many faces, and many naked feet, and many wooden shoes. Those who had been greedy with the staves of the cask, had acquired a tigerish smear about the mouth; and one tall joker so besmirched scrawled upon a wall with his finger dipped in muddy wine-lees—BLOOD.

The time was to come, when that wine too would be spilled on the street-stones, and when the stain of it would be red upon many there.

Across the streets, at wide intervals, one clumsy lamp was slung by a rope and pulley; at night, when the lamplighter had let these down, and lighted, and hoisted them again, a feeble grove of dim wicks swung in a sickly manner overhead, as if they were at sea. Indeed they were at sea, and the ship and crew were in peril of tempest.

For, the time was to come, when the gaunt scarecrows of that region should have watched the lamplighter, in their idleness and hunger, so long, as to conceive the idea of improving on his method, and hauling up men by those ropes and pulleys. But, the time was not come yet.

The wine-shop was a corner shop, better than most others in its appearance and degree, and the master of the wine-shop had stood outside it, looking on at the struggle for the lost wine. 'It's not my affair,' said he, with a final shrug of the shoulders. 'The people from the market did it. Let them bring another.'

Then, his eyes happening to catch the tall joker writing up his joke, he called to him across the way:

'Say, then, my Gaspard, what do you do there?'

The fellow pointed to his joke with immense significance.

'What now? Are you a subject for the mad hospital?' said the wine-shop keeper, crossing the road, and obliterating the jest with a handful of mud. 'Why do you write in the public streets? Call wine, wine; and finish there.' With that advice, he wiped his soiled hand upon the joker's dress, such as it was—quite deliberately, as having dirtied the hand on his account; and then re-crossed the road and entered the wine-shop.

This wine-shop keeper was a bull-necked man of thirty, who wore no coat, but carried one slung over his shoulder. His shirt-sleeves were rolled up, too, and his brown arms were bare to the elbows. He was a dark man, with good eyes and a good bold breadth between them. Good-humoured-looking on the whole, but implacable-looking too; evidently a man of strong resolution and a set purpose.

Madame Defarge, his wife, sat in the shop behind the counter as he came in. Madame Defarge was a stout woman of about his own age, with a watchful eye that seldom seemed to look at anything. There was a character about Madame Defarge, from which one might have predicted that she did not often make mistakes. Her knitting was before her, but she had laid it down to pick her teeth with a toothpick. Thus engaged, Madame Defarge said nothing when her lord came in, but coughed just one grain of cough. This suggested to her husband that he would do well to look round the shop among the customers, for any new customer who had dropped in while he stepped over the way.

An elderly gentleman and a young lady were seated in a corner. Other company were there: two playing cards, two playing dominoes, three standing by the counter. As he passed behind the counter, he took notice that the elderly gentleman said in a look to the young lady, 'This is our man.'

But he feigned not to notice the two strangers, and joined the three customers who were drinking at the counter.

'How goes it, Jacques?' said one of these three to Monsieur Defarge. 'Is all the spilt wine swallowed?'

'Every drop, Jacques,' answered Monsieur Defarge.

When this interchange of christian name was effected, Madame Defarge, picking her teeth with her toothpick, coughed another grain of cough.

'It is not often,' said the second of the three, addressing Monsieur Defarge, 'that many of these miserable beasts know the taste of wine, or of anything but black bread and death. Is it not so, Jacques?'

'It is so, Jacques,' Monsieur Defarge returned.

At this second interchange of the christian name, Madame Defarge, still using her toothpick with profound composure, coughed another grain of cough.

The last of the three now said his say, as he put down his empty drinking vessel.

'Ah! So much the worse! A bitter taste it is that such poor cattle always have in their mouths, and hard lives they live, Jacques. Am I right, Jacques?'

'You are right, Jacques,' was the response of Monsieur Defarge.

The third interchange of the christian name was completed at the moment when Madame Defarge put her toothpick by, and slightly rustled in her seat.

'True!' muttered her husband. 'Gentlemen—my wife!'

The three customers pulled off their hats to Madame Defarge. She replied by bending her head, and giving them a quick look. Then she glanced in a casual manner round the wine-shop, took up her knitting with great apparent calmness, and became absorbed in it.

'Gentlemen,' said her husband, who had kept his bright eye observantly upon her, 'good-day. The chamber, furnished bachelor-fashion, that you wished to see, and were inquiring for when I stepped out, is on the fifth floor. The doorway of the staircase gives on the little court-yard close to the left here.'

They paid for their wine, and left the place. The eyes of Monsieur Defarge were studying his wife at her knitting when the elderly gentleman advanced from his corner, and begged the favour of a word.

'Willingly, sir,' said Monsieur Defarge, and quietly stepped with him to the door.

Their conference was very short. Almost at the first word, Monsieur Defarge started, nodded and went out. The gentleman then beckoned to the young lady, and they, too, went out. Madame Defarge knitted with nimble fingers, and saw nothing.

Mr. Jarvis Lorry and Miss Manette, emerging from the

wine-shop thus, joined Monsieur Defarge in the doorway to which he had directed his other company just before. In the entry to the gloomy tile-paved staircase, Monsieur Defarge bent down on one knee to the child of his old master, and put her hand to his lips. It was a gentle action, but not at all gently done; a very remarkable transformation had come over him in a few seconds. He had become a secret, angry, dangerous man.

As they began ascending the stairs, Mr. Lorry whispered:

'He is greatly changed?'

'Changed!'

The keeper of the wine-shop stopped to strike the wall with his left hand, and muttered a tremendous curse. No direct answer could have been half so forcible. Mr. Lorry's spirits grew heavier and heavier, as he and his two companions ascended higher and higher.

Through the rusted bars, glimpses were caught of the jumbled neighbourhood; and nothing within range, nearer than the summits of the two great towers of Notre-Dame, had any promise in it of healthy life. At last, the garret story was reached. The keeper of the wine-shop turned here, and took out a key.

'The door is locked then, my friend?' said Mr. Lorry, surprised.

'Ay. Yes,' was the grim reply of Monsieur Defarge.

'You think it necessary to keep the unfortunate gentleman so retired?'

'I think it necessary to turn the key.'

'Why?'

'Why! Because he has lived so long, locked up, that he would be frightened—rave—tear himself to pieces—die—come to I know not what harm—if his door was left open.'

'Is it possible?' exclaimed Mr. Lorry.

'Is it possible?' repeated Defarge, bitterly. 'Yes. And a beautiful world we live in, when it *is* possible. Long live the Devil. Let us go on.'

This dialogue had been held in so very low a whisper, that not a word of it had reached the young lady's ears. But, by this time she trembled under such strong emotion, and her face expressed such deep anxiety, and, above all, such dread and terror, that Mr. Lorry said:

'Courage, dear miss! Courage! Business! The worst will be over in a moment; it is but passing the room-door, and the worst is over. Then, all the good you bring to him, all the relief, all the happiness you bring to him, begin. Come, now. Business, business!'

Round an abrupt turn, they came all at once in sight of three men, intently looking into a room through some chinks or holes in the wall. They were the three of one name who had been drinking in the wine-shop.

'I forgot them in the surprise of your visit,' explained Monsieur Defarge. 'Leave us, good boys; we have business here.'

The three glided by, and went silently down.

Mr. Lorry asked in a whisper, with a little anger:

'Do you make a show of Monsieur Manette?'

'I show him, in the way you have seen, to a chosen few.'

'Who are the few? How do you choose them?'

'I choose them as real men, of my name—Jacques is my name—to whom the sight is likely to do good.' He stooped, and looked in through the crevice in the wall, then struck twice or thrice upon the door—evidently with no other object than to make a noise there. With the same intention, he drew the key across it, three or four times, before he put it clumsily into the lock, and turned it as heavily as he could.

The door slowly opened inward under his hand, and he looked into the room and said something. A faint voice answered something.

He looked back over his shoulder, and beckoned them to enter. Mr. Lorry got his arm securely round the daughter's waist, and held her; for he felt that she was sinking.

'A—a—a—business, business!' he urged, with a moisture that was not of business shining on his cheek. 'Come in, come in!'

The garret, built to be a depository for firewood and the like, was dim, and it was difficult, on first coming in, to see anything; and long habit alone could have slowly formed in anyone, the ability to do any work requiring nicety in such obscurity. Yet, work of that kind was being done in the garret; for, with his back towards the door, and his face towards the window, a white-haired man sat on a low bench, stooping forward and very busy, making shoes.

---

3 · THE SHOEMAKER

'Good day!' said Monsieur Defarge, looking down at the white head that bent low over the shoemaking.

It was raised for a moment, and a very faint voice responded:

'Good day!'

'You are still at work, I see?'

After a long silence, the head was lifted for another moment, and the voice replied, 'Yes—I am working.' The faintness of the voice was pitiable and dreadful.

'Are you going to finish that pair of shoes to-day?' asked Defarge, motioning to Mr. Lorry to come forward.

'What did you say?'

'Do you mean to finish that pair of shoes to-day?'

'I can't say that I mean to. I suppose so. I don't know.'

But, the question reminded him of his work, and he bent over it again.

Mr. Lorry came silently forward, leaving the daughter by the door. When he had stood, for a minute or two, by the side of Defarge, the shoemaker looked up. He showed no surprise at seeing another figure, but the unsteady fingers of one of his hands strayed to his lips as he looked at it (his lips and his nails were of the same pale lead-colour), and then the hand dropped to his work, and he once more bent over the shoe. The look and the action had occupied but an instant.

'You have a visitor, you see,' said Monsieur Defarge.

'What did you say?'

'Here is a visitor.'

The shoemaker looked up as before, but without removing a hand from his work.

'Come!' said Defarge. 'Here is monsieur, who knows a well-made shoe when he sees one. Show him that shoe you are working at. Take it, monsieur.'

Mr. Lorry took it in his hand.

'Tell monsieur what kind of shoe it is, and the maker's name.'

There was a longer pause than usual, before the shoemaker replied:

'It is a lady's shoe. It is a young lady's walking-shoe. It is in the present mode. I never saw the mode. I have had a pattern in my hand.' He glanced at the shoe with some little passing touch of pride.

'And the maker's name?' said Defarge.

Now that he had no work to hold, he laid the knuckles of the right hand in the hollow of the left, and then the knuckles of the left hand in the hollow of the right, and then passed a hand across his bearded chin, and so on in regular changes, without a moment's intermission.

'Did you ask me for my name?'

'Assuredly I did.'

'One Hundred and Five, North Tower.'

'Is that all?'

'One Hundred and Five, North Tower.'

'You are not a shoemaker by trade?' said Mr. Lorry, looking steadfastly at him.

His haggard eyes turned to Defarge as if he would have transferred the question to him: but as no help came from that quarter, they turned back on the questioner.

'I am not a shoemaker by trade? No, I was not a shoemaker by trade. I—I learnt it here. I taught myself. I asked leave to——'

He lapsed away, even for minutes, ringing those measured changes on his hands the whole time. His eyes came slowly back, at last, to the face from which they had wandered.

'I asked leave to teach myself, and I got it with much difficulty after a long while, and I have made shoes ever since.'

As he held out his hand for the shoe that had been taken from him, Mr. Lorry said, still looking steadfastly in his face:

'Monsieur Manette, do you remember nothing of me?'

The shoe dropped to the ground, and he sat looking fixedly at the questioner.

'Monsieur Manette'—Mr. Lorry laid his hand upon Defarge's arm—'do you remember nothing of this man?

Look at him. Look at me. Is there no old banker, no old business, no old servant, no old time, rising in your mind, Monsieur Manette?'

As the captive of many years sat looking fixedly, by turns, at Mr. Lorry and at Defarge, some long obliterated marks of an actively intent intelligence in the middle of the forehead, gradually forced themselves through the black mist that had fallen on him. They were overclouded again, they were fainter, they were gone; but they had been there. Finally, with a deep long sigh, he took the shoe up, and resumed his work.

'Have you recognized him, monsieur?' asked Defarge in a whisper.

'Yes; for a moment. At first I thought it quite hopeless, but I have unquestionably seen, for a single moment, the face that I once knew so well. Hush! Let us draw further back. Hush!'

She had moved from the wall of the garret, very near to the bench on which he sat. There was something awful in his unconsciousness of the figure that could have put out its hand and touched him as he stooped over his labour.

Not a word was spoken, not a sound was made. She stood, like a spirit, beside him, and he bent over his work.

It happened, at length, that he had occasion to change the instrument in his hand, for his shoemaker's knife. He had taken it up, and was stooping to work again, when his eyes caught the skirt of her dress. He raised them, and saw her face.

He stared at her with a fearful look, and after a while his lips began to form some words, though no sound proceeded from them. By degrees, in the pauses of his quick and laboured breathing, he was heard to say:

'Who are you?'

Not yet trusting the tones of her voice, she sat down on the bench beside him. He recoiled, but she laid her hand upon his arm. A strange thrill struck him when she did so, and visibly passed over his frame; he laid the knife down softly, as he sat staring at her.

Her golden hair, which she wore in long curls, had been hurriedly pushed aside, and fell down over her neck. Advancing his hand by little and little, he took it up and looked at it. In the midst of the action he went astray, and, with another deep sigh, fell to work at his shoemaking.

But not for long. Releasing his arm, she laid her hand upon his shoulder. After looking doubtfully at it, two or three times, as if to be sure that it was really there, he laid down his work.

'She laid her head upon my shoulder, that night when I was summoned out—she had a fear of my going, though I had none.—No, no; you are too young, too blooming.—No, no. She was—before the slow years of the North Tower—ages ago.'

At his softened tone and manner, his daughter fell upon her knees before him, with her appealing hands upon his breast. His cold white head mingled with her radiant hair, which warmed and lighted it as though it were the light of freedom shining on him. She held him close round the neck, and rocked him like a child.

When the quiet of the garret had been long undisturbed, and his heaving breast and shaken form had long yielded to the calm that must follow all storms, they came forward to raise the father and daughter from the ground. He had gradually dropped to the floor, and lay there in a lethargy, worn out. She had nestled down with him, that his head might lie upon her arm; and her hair drooping over him curtained him from the light.

'If, without disturbing him,' she said, 'all could be arranged for our leaving Paris at once, so that, from the very door, he could be taken away——'

'But, consider. Is he fit for the journey?' asked Mr. Lorry.

'More fit for that, I think, than to remain in this city, so dreadful to him.'

'It is true,' said Defarge, who was kneeling to look on and hear. 'More than that; Monsieur Manette is, for all reasons, best out of France. Say, shall I hire a carriage and post-horses?'

'That's business,' said Mr. Lorry, resuming on the shortest notice his methodical manners; 'and if business is to be done, I had better do it.'

'Then be so kind,' urged Miss Manette, 'as to leave us here. You see how composed he has become, and you cannot be afraid to leave him with me now. If you will lock the door to secure us from interruption, I do not doubt that you will find him, when you come back, as quiet as you leave him.'

Both Mr. Lorry and Defarge were rather disinclined to this course, and in favour of one of them remaining. But, as there were not only carriage and horses to be seen to, but travelling papers; and as time pressed, for the day was drawing to an end, it came at last to their hastily dividing the business that was necessary to be done, and hurrying away to do it.

Then, as the darkness closed in, the daughter laid her head down on the hard ground close at the father's side, and watched him. The darkness deepened and deepened, and they both lay quiet, until a light gleamed through the chinks in the wall.

Mr. Lorry and Monsieur Defarge had made all ready for the journey, and had brought with them, besides travelling cloaks and wrappers, bread and meat, wine, and hot coffee. Monsieur Defarge put this provender, and the lamp he carried, on the shoemakers' bench (there was nothing else in the garret but a pallet bed), and he and Mr. Lorry roused the captive, and assisted him to his feet.

In the submissive way of one long accustomed to obey, he ate and drank what they gave him, and put on the cloak and other wrappings, that they gave him to wear. He readily responded to his daughter's drawing her arm through his, and took—and kept—her hand in both his own.

They began to descend; Monsieur Defarge going first with the lamp, Mr. Lorry closing the little procession. They had not traversed many steps of the long main staircase when the old man stopped, and stared at the roof and round at the walls.

That he had no recollection whatever of his having been brought from his prison to that house, was apparent to them. They heard him mutter, 'One Hundred and Five, North Tower'; and when he looked about him, it evidently was for the strong fortress-walls which had long encompassed him. On their reaching the court-yard he instinctively altered his tread, as being in expectation of a drawbridge; and when there was no drawbridge, and he saw the carriage waiting in the open street, he dropped his daughter's hand and clasped his head.

No crowd was about the door; no people were discernible at any of the many windows; not even a chance passer-by was in the street. Only one soul was to be seen, and that was

Madame Defarge—who leaned against the door-post, knitting, and saw nothing.

The prisoner had got into the coach, and his daughter had followed him, when Mr. Lorry's feet were arrested on the step by his asking, miserably, for his shoemaking tools and the unfinished shoes. Madame Defarge immediately called to her husband that she would get them, and went knitting, out of the lamplight, through the court-yard. She quickly brought them down and handed them in;—and immediately afterwards leaned against the door-post, knitting, and saw nothing.

Defarge got upon the box, and gave the word 'To the Barrier!' The postilion cracked his whip, and they clattered away under the feeble over-swinging lamps.

Under the over-swinging lamps and by lighted shops, gay crowds, illuminated coffee-houses, and theatre-doors, to one of the city gates. Soldiers with lanterns, at the guard-house there. 'Your papers, travellers!'

'See here then, Monsieur the Officer,' said Defarge, getting down, and taking him gravely apart, 'these are the papers of monsieur inside, with the white head. They were consigned to me, with him, at the——' He dropped his voice, there was a flutter among the military lanterns, and one of them being handed into the coach by an arm in uniform, the eyes connected with the arm looked, not an every-day or an every-night look, at monsieur with the white head. 'It is well. Forward!' from the uniform. 'Adieu!' from Defarge. And so, under a short grove of feebler and feebler over-swinging lamps, out under the great grove of stars.

4 · FIVE YEARS LATER

TELLSON'S BANK by Temple Bar was an old-fashioned place, even in the year one thousand seven hundred and eighty.

Cramped in all kinds of dim cupboards and hutches at Tellson's, the oldest of men carried on the business gravely. When they took a young man into Tellson's London house, they hid him somewhere till he was old. They kept him in a dark place, like a cheese, until he had the full Tellson flavour and blue-mould upon him.

Outside Tellson's—never by any means in it, unless called in—was an odd-job-man, an occasional porter and messenger. People understood that Tellson's, in a stately way, tolerated the odd-job-man. The house had always tolerated some person in that capacity, and time and tide had drifted this person to the post. His name was Jerry Cruncher.

Encamped at a quarter to nine, in good time to touch his three-cornered hat to the oldest of men as they passed in to Tellson's, Jerry took up his station on a windy March morning. Presently the head of one of the regular indoor messengers attached to Tellson's was put through the door, and the word was given.

'Porter wanted!'

'You know the Old Bailey criminal courts well, no doubt?' said one of the oldest of clerks to Jerry the messenger.

'Ye-es, sir,' returned Jerry, in something of a dogged manner. 'I *do* know the Bailey.'

'Just so. And you know Mr. Lorry.'

'I know Mr. Lorry, sir, much better than I know the Bailey. Much better,' said Jerry.

'Very well. Find the door where the witnesses go in, and show the door-keeper this note for Mr. Lorry. He will then let you in.'

'Am I to wait in the court, sir?'

'I am going to tell you. The door-keeper will pass the note to Mr. Lorry, and do you make any gesture that will attract Mr. Lorry's attention, and show him where you stand. Then what you have to do is, to remain there until he wants you.'

'Is that all, sir?'

'That's all. He wishes to have a messenger at hand. This is to tell him you are there.'

As the ancient clerk deliberately folded and superscribed the note, Mr. Cruncher, after surveying him in silence until he came to the blotting-paper stage, remarked:

'I suppose they'll be trying Forgeries this morning?'

'Treason!'

Jerry took the letter, made his bow, and went his way. Making his way through the crowd at the court, the messenger found the door he sought, and handed in his letter through a trap in it.

After some delay and demur, the door grudgingly turned on its hinges a very little way, and allowed Mr. Jerry Cruncher to squeeze himself into court.

'What's on?' he asked, in a whisper, of the man he found himself next to.

'Nothing yet.'

'What's coming on?'

'The Treason case.'

Mr. Cruncher's attention was here diverted to the door-keeper, whom he saw making his way to Mr. Lorry, with the note in his hand. Mr. Lorry sat at a table, among the gentlemen in wigs: not far from a wigged gentleman, the prisoner's counsel, who had a great bundle of papers before him: and nearly opposite another wigged gentleman with his hands in his pockets, whose whole attention, when Mr. Cruncher looked at him then or afterwards, seemed to be concentrated on the ceiling of the court. After some gruff coughing and rubbing of his chin and signing with his hand, Jerry attracted the notice of Mr. Lorry, who had stood up to look for him, and who quietly nodded and sat down again.

Presently, the dock became the central point of interest. Two gaolers, who had been standing there, went out, and the prisoner was brought in, and put to the bar. Everybody present, except the one wigged gentleman who looked at the ceiling, stared at him. The object of all this staring was a young man of about five-and-twenty, well-grown and well-looking, with a sunburnt cheek and a dark eye. He was plainly dressed in black, and his hair, which was long and dark, was gathered in a ribbon at the back of his neck; more to be out of his way than for ornament. He was pale, but otherwise quite self-possessed, bowed to the Judge, and stood quiet.

Silence in the court! Charles Darnay had yesterday pleaded Not Guilty to an indictment denouncing him (with infinite jingle and jangle) for that he was a false traitor to our serene, illustrious, excellent, and so forth, prince, our Lord the King, by reason of his having, on divers occasions, and by divers means and ways, assisted Lewis, the French King, in his wars against our said serene, illustrious, excellent, and so forth; and so forth; that was to say, by coming and going, between the dominions of our said serene, illustrious, excellent, and so forth, and those of the said French Lewis, and wickedly, falsely, traitorously, and otherwise evil-adverbiously, revealing to the said French Lewis what forces our said serene, illustrious, excellent, and so forth, had in preparation to send to Canada and North America. This much, Jerry made out with huge satisfaction, and so arrived at the understanding that the aforesaid, and over and over again aforesaid, Charles Darnay, stood there before him upon his trial; that the jury were swearing in; and that Mr. Attorney-General was making ready to speak.

The accused, who was (and who knew he was) being mentally hanged, beheaded, and quartered, by everybody there, neither flinched from the situation, nor assumed any theatrical air in it. He was quiet and attentive; watched the opening proceedings with a grave interest; and stood with his hands resting on the slab of wood before him.

It happened that he turned his face to that side of the court which was on his left. About on a level with his eyes, there sat, in that corner of the Judge's bench, two persons upon whom his look immediately rested; he looked so keenly, that all the eyes that were turned upon him, turned to them.

The spectators saw in the two figures, a young lady of little more than twenty, and a gentleman who was evidently her father; a man of a very remarkable appearance in respect of the absolute whiteness of his hair, and a certain indescribable intensity of face, but pondering and self-communing. When this expression was upon him, he looked as if he were old; but when it was stirred and broken up—as it was now, in a moment, on his speaking to his daughter—he became a handsome man, not past the prime of life.

His daughter had one of her hands drawn through his arm. She had drawn close to him, in her dread of the scene, and in her pity for the prisoner. Her forehead had been strikingly expressive of an engrossing compassion that saw nothing but the peril of the accused. This had been so very noticeable, that starers who had had no pity for him were touched by her; and the whisper went about, 'Who are they?'

'Witnesses.'

'For which side?'

'Against.'

'Against what side?'

'The prisoner's.'

The Judge, whose eyes had gone in the general direction, recalled them, leaned back in his seat, and looked steadily at the man whose life was in his hand, as Mr. Attorney-General rose to spin the rope, grind the axe, and hammer the nails into the scaffold.

Mr. Attorney-General had to inform the jury, that the prisoner before them, though young in years, was old in the treasonable practices which claimed the forfeit of his life. That, it was certain the prisoner had for long been in the habit of passing and repassing between France and England, on secret business of which he could give no honest account. That, Providence had put it into the heart of a person who was beyond fear and beyond reproach, to ferret out the nature of the prisoner's schemes, and, struck with horror, to disclose them to his Majesty's Chief Secretary of State. That, this patriot would be produced before them. That, he had been the prisoner's friend, but, detecting his infamy, had resolved to denounce him. That, the lofty example of this immaculate and unimpeachable witness for the Crown, to refer to whom however unworthily was an honour, had communicated itself to the prisoner's servant, and had engendered in him a holy determination to examine his master's table-drawers and pockets, and secrete his papers.

That, the evidence of these two witnesses, coupled with the documents of their discovering that would be produced, would show the prisoner to have been furnished with lists of his Majesty's forces, and of their disposition and preparation, both by sea and land, and would leave no doubt that he had habitually conveyed such information to a hostile power. That, these lists could not be proved to be in the prisoner's handwriting; but that it was all the same; that, indeed, it was rather the better for the prosecution, as showing the prisoner to be artful in his precautions. That, the proof would go back five years, and would show the prisoner already engaged in these pernicious missions, within a few weeks before the date of the very first action fought between the British troops and the Americans. That, for these reasons, the jury, being a loyal jury (as he knew they were), and being a responsible jury (as *they* knew they were), must positively find the prisoner Guilty, and make an end of him, whether they liked it or not.

When the Attorney-General ceased, a buzz arose in the court, as the unimpeachable patriot appeared in the witness-box. Mr. Solicitor-General then examined the patriot: John Barsad, gentleman, by name. His story was exactly what Mr. Attorney-General had described it to be—perhaps, if it had a fault, a little too exactly. Having released his noble bosom of its burden, he would have modestly withdrawn himself, but that the wigged gentleman with the papers before him, sitting not far from Mr. Lorry, begged to ask him a few questions. The wigged gentleman sitting opposite, still looked at the ceiling of the court.

Had he ever been a spy himself? No, he scorned the base insinuation. What did he live upon? His property. Where was his property? He didn't precisely remember where it was. What was it? No business of anybody's. Had he inherited it? Yes, he had. From whom? Distant relation. Very distant? Rather. Ever been in prison? Certainly not. Never in a debtors' prison? Didn't see what that had to do with it. Never in a debtors' prison?—Come, once again. Never? Yes. How many times? Two or three times. Not five or six? Perhaps. Of what profession? Gentleman. Ever been kicked? Might have been. Frequently? No. Ever kicked downstairs? Decidedly not; once received a kick on the top of a staircase, and fell down-stairs of his own accord. Kicked on that occasion for cheating at dice? Something to that effect was said by the intoxicated liar who committed the assault, but it was not true. Ever borrow money of the prisoner? Yes. Ever pay him? No. Was not this intimacy with the prisoner, in reality a very slight one, forced upon the prisoner in coaches, inns, and packets? No. Sure he saw the prisoner with these lists? Certain. Knew no more about the lists? No. Had not procured them himself, for instance? No. Expect to get anything by this evidence? No. Not in regular government pay and employment, to lay traps? Oh dear no. Or to do anything? Oh dear no. Swear that? Over and over again.

The virtuous servant, Roger Cly, swore his way through the case at a great rate. He had taken service with the prisoner, in good faith and simplicity, four years ago. He had asked the prisoner, aboard the Calais packet, if he wanted a handy fellow, and the prisoner had engaged him. He had not asked the prisoner to take the handy fellow as an act of charity—never thought of such a thing. He began to have suspicions of the prisoner, and to keep an eye upon him, soon afterwards. In arranging his clothes, while travelling, he had seen similar lists to these in the prisoner's pockets, over and over again. He had taken these lists from the drawer of the prisoner's desk. He had not put them there first. He had never been suspected of stealing a silver tea-pot; he had been maligned respecting a mustard-pot, but it turned out to be only a plated one. He had known the last witness seven or eight years; that was merely a coincidence. He didn't call it a particularly curious coincidence; most coincidences were curious.

Mr. Attorney-General called Mr. Jarvis Lorry.

'Mr. Jarvis Lorry, are you a clerk in Tellson's Bank?'

'I am.'

'On a certain Friday night in November one thousand seven hundred and seventy-five, did business occasion you to travel between London and Dover by the mail?'

'It did.'

'Were there any other passengers in the mail?'

'Two.'

'Did they alight on the road in the course of the night?'

'They did.'

'Mr. Lorry, look upon the prisoner. Was he one of those two passengers?'

'I cannot say that he was.'

'Does he resemble either of those two passengers?'

'Both were so wrapped up, and the night was so dark, and we were all so reserved, that I cannot say even that.'

'Mr. Lorry, look again upon the prisoner. Supposing him wrapped up as those two passengers were, is there anything in his bulk and stature to render it unlikely that he was one of them?'

'No.'

'You will not swear, Mr. Lorry, that he was not one of them?'

'No.'

'So at least you say he may have been one of them?'

'Yes. Except that I remember them both to have been—like myself—timorous of highwaymen, and the prisoner has not a timorous air.'

'Mr. Lorry, look once more upon the prisoner. Have you seen him, to your certain knowledge, before?'

'I have.'

'When?'

'I was returning from France a few days afterwards, and, at Calais, the prisoner came on board the packet-ship in which I returned, and made the voyage with me.'

'Were you travelling alone, Mr. Lorry, or with any companion?'

'With two companions. A gentleman and lady. They are here.'

'They are here. Had you any conversation with the prisoner?'

'Hardly any. The weather was stormy, and the passage long and rough, and I lay on a sofa, almost from shore to shore.'

'Miss Manette!'

The young lady, to whom all eyes had been turned before, and were now turned again, stood up where she had sat. Her father rose with her, and kept her hand drawn through his arm.

'Miss Manette, look upon the prisoner.'

To be confronted with such pity, and such earnest youth and beauty, was far more trying to the accused than to be confronted with all the crowd.

'Miss Manette, have you seen the prisoner before?'

'Yes, sir.'

'Where and when?'

'On board of the packet-ship just now referred to, sir, and on the same occasion.'

'You are the young lady just now referred to?'

'O! most unhappily, I am!'

The plaintive tone of her compassion merged into the less musical voice of the Judge, as he said, something fiercely: 'Answer the questions put to you, and make no remark upon them.'

'Miss Manette, had you any conversation with the prisoner on that passage across the Channel?'

'Yes, sir.'

'Recall it.'

In the midst of a profound stillness, she faintly began:

'When the gentleman came on board——'

'Do you mean the prisoner?' inquired the Judge, knitting his brows.

'Yes, my Lord.'

'Then say the prisoner.'

'When the prisoner came on board, he noticed that my father,' turning her eyes lovingly to him as he stood beside her, 'was much fatigued and in a very weak state of health. My father was so reduced that I was afraid to take him out of the air, and I had made a bed for him on the deck near the cabin steps, and I sat on the deck at his side to take care of him. There were no other passengers that night, but we four. The prisoner was so good as to advise me how I could shelter my father from the wind and weather, better than I had done. He expressed great gentleness and kindness for my father's state, and I am sure he felt it. That was the manner of our beginning to speak together.'

'Let me interrupt you for a moment. Had he come on board alone?'

'No.'

'How many were with him?'

'Two French gentlemen.'

'Had they conferred together?'

'They had conferred together until the last moment, when it was necessary for the French gentlemen to be landed in their boat.'

'Had any papers been handed about among them, similar to these lists?'

'Some papers had been handed about among them, but I don't know what papers.'

'Like these in shape and size?'

'Possibly, but indeed I don't know.'

'Now, to the prisoner's conversation, Miss Manette.'

'The prisoner was as open in his confidence with me as he was kind, and good, and useful to my father. I hope,' bursting into tears, 'I may not repay him by doing him harm to-day.'

'Miss Manette, if the prisoner does not perfectly understand that you give the evidence which it is your duty to give, with great unwillingness, he is the only person present in that condition. Please to go on.'

'He told me that he was travelling on business of a delicate and difficult nature, which might get people into trouble, and that he was therefore travelling under an assumed name. He said that this business had, within a few days, taken him to France, and might, at intervals, take him backwards and forwards between France and England for a long time to come.'

Mr. Attorney-General now signified to my Lord, that he deemed it necessary, as a matter of precaution and form, to call the young lady's father, Doctor Manette. Who was called accordingly.

'Doctor Manette, look upon the prisoner. Have you ever seen him before?'

'Once. When he called at my lodgings in London, some three years, or three years and a half ago.'

'Can you identify him as your fellow-passenger on board the packet, or speak to his conversation with your daughter?'

'Sir, I can do neither.'

'Is there any particular and special reason for your being unable to do either?'

He answered, in a low voice, 'There is.'

'Has it been your misfortune to undergo a long imprisonment, without trial, or even accusation, in your native country, Doctor Manette?'

He answered, in a tone that went to every heart, 'A long imprisonment.'

'Were you newly released on the occasion in question?'

'They tell me so.'

'Have you no remembrance of the occasion?'

'None. My mind is a blank, from some time—I cannot even say what time—when I employed myself, in my captivity, in making shoes, to the time when I found myself living in London with my dear daughter here.'

Mr. Attorney-General sat down, and the father and daughter sat down together.

A singular circumstance then arose in the case. The object in hand being to show that the prisoner went down in the Dover mail on that Friday night in November five years ago, and got out of the mail in the night, as a blind, at a place where he did not remain, but from which he travelled back some dozen miles or more, to a garrison and dockyard town, and there collected information; a witness was called to identify him as having been at the precise time required, in the coffee-room of an hotel in that garrison-and-dockyard town, waiting for another person. The prisoner's counsel was cross-examining this witness with no result, except that he had never seen the prisoner on any other occasion, when the wigged gentleman who had all this time been looking at the ceiling of the court, wrote a word or two on a little piece of paper, screwed it up, and tossed it to him. Opening this piece of paper in the next pause, the counsel looked with great attention and curiosity at the prisoner.

'You say again you are quite sure that it *was* the prisoner?'

The witness was quite sure.

'Did you ever see anybody very like the prisoner?'

Not so like (the witness said) as that he could be mistaken.

'Look well upon that gentleman, my learned friend there,' pointing to him who had tossed the paper over, 'and then look well upon the prisoner. How say you? Are they very like each other?'

Allowing for my learned friend's appearance being careless and slovenly if not debauched, they were sufficiently like each other to surprise, not only the witness, but everybody present, when they were thus brought into comparison. My Lord being prayed to bid my learned friend lay aside his wig, the likeness became much more remarkable. My Lord inquired of Mr. Stryver (the prisoner's counsel), whether they were next to try Mr. Carton (name of my learned friend) for treason? But Mr. Stryver replied to my Lord, no; but he would ask the witness to tell him whether what happened once, might happen twice; whether he would have been so confident if he had seen this illustration of his rashness sooner. The result of this was, to smash this witness and to shiver his part of the case.

Mr. Stryver fitted the prisoner's case on the jury, like a compact suit of clothes; showing them how the patriot, Barsad, was a hired spy and traitor, an unblushing trafficker in blood, and one of the greatest scoundrels upon earth. How the virtuous servant, Cly, was his friend and partner, and was worthy to be; how the watchful eyes of those forgers and false swearers had rested on the prisoner as a victim, because some family affairs in France, he being of French extraction, did require his making those passages across the Channel. How the evidence that had been warped and wrested from the young lady, whose anguish in giving it they had witnessed, came to nothing.

Mr. Stryver then called his few witnesses. Mr. Attorney-General followed, showing how Barsad and Cly were even a hundred times better than he had thought them, and the prisoner a hundred times worse. Lastly came my Lord himself, summing up, not by any means in the prisoner's favour. And now, the jury turned to consider, and the court buzzed again.

Mr. Carton had so long sat with his hands in his pockets, and his eyes on the ceiling as they had been all day. Something especially reckless in his demeanour gave him a disreputable look; yet this Mr. Carton took in more details of the scene than he appeared to take in; for now, when Miss Manette's head dropped upon her father's breast, he was the first to see it, and to say audibly: 'Officer! look to that young lady. Help the gentleman to take her out. Don't you see she will fall!'

There was much commiseration for her as she was removed, and much sympathy with her father. It had evidently been a great distress to him, to have the days of his imprisonment recalled.

As they passed out, the jury, who had turned back and paused a moment, spoke, through their foreman.

They were not agreed, and wished to retire. My Lord showed some surprise that they were not agreed, but signified his pleasure that they should retire under watch and ward, and retired himself. The trial had lasted all day, and the lamps in the court were now being lighted.

Mr. Lorry, who had gone out when the young lady and her father went out, now reappeared, and beckoned to Jerry.

'Jerry, if you wish to take something to eat, you can. But, keep in the way. You will be sure to hear when the jury come in. Don't be a moment behind them, for I want you to take the verdict back to the bank.'

Jerry had just enough forehead to knuckle, and he knuckled it in acknowledgment of this communication and a shilling. Mr. Carton came up at the moment, and touched Mr. Lorry on the arm.

'How is the young lady?'

'She is greatly distressed; but her father is comforting her, and she feels the better for being out of court.'

'I'll tell the prisoner so. It won't do for a respectable bank gentleman like you, to be seen speaking to him publicly, you know.'

Mr. Lorry reddened as if he were conscious of having debated the point in his mind, and Mr. Carton made his way to the outside of the bar.

'Mr. Darnay!'

The prisoner came forward.

'You will naturally be anxious to hear of the witness, Miss Manette. She will do very well. You have seen the worst of her agitation.'

'I am deeply sorry to have been the cause of it. Could you tell her so for me, with my fervent acknowledgments?'

'Yes, I could. I will, if you ask it.'

Mr. Carton's manner was so careless as to be almost insolent. He stood, half turned from the prisoner, lounging with his elbow against the bar.

'I do ask it. Accept my cordial thanks.'

'What,' said Carton, still only half turned towards him, 'do you expect, Mr. Darnay?'

'The worst.'

'It's the wisest thing to expect, and the likeliest. But I think their withdrawing is in your favour.'

An hour and a half limped heavily away. The messenger, uncomfortably settled on a form, had dropped into a doze, when a loud murmur and a rapid tide of people setting up the stairs that led to the court, carried him along with them.

'Jerry! Jerry!' Mr. Lorry was already calling at the door when he got there.

'Here, sir! It's a fight to get back again. Here I am, sir.'

Mr. Lorry handed him a paper through the throng. 'Quick! Have you got it?'

'Yes, sir!'

Hastily written on the paper was the word 'ACQUITTED'.

---

5 · THE JACKAL

FROM the dimly-lighted passages of the court, the last sediment of the human stew that had been boiling there all day, was straining off, when Doctor Manette, Lucie Manette, his daughter, Mr. Lorry, the solicitor for the defence, and its counsel, Mr. Stryver, stood gathered round Mr. Charles Darnay, congratulating him on his escape from death.

It would have been difficult by a far brighter light, to recognize in Doctor Manette, intellectual of face and upright of bearing, the shoemaker of the garret in Paris. Yet, there was an abstraction that overclouded him fitfully, without any apparent reason.

Mr. Stryver, stout, loud, red, bluff, and free from any drawback of delicacy, had a pushing way of shouldering himself (morally and physically) into companies and conversations, that argued well for his shouldering his way up in life. He still wore his wig and gown, and he said, squaring himself at his late client, and squeezing the innocent Mr. Lorry clean out of the group: 'I am glad to have brought you off with honour, Mr. Darnay. It was an infamous prosecution, grossly infamous; but not the less likely to succeed on that account.'

'You have laid me under an obligation to you for life—in two senses,' said his late client, taking his hand.

'I have done my best for you, Mr. Darnay; and my best is as good as another man's, I believe.'

The friends of the acquitted prisoner dispersed, under the impression—which he himself had originated—that he would not be released that night. But Darnay found himself free, and alone, except for Carton, who smelt of port wine and did not appear to be quite sober. He turned to Darnay:

'This is a strange chance that throws you and me together. This must be a strange night to you, standing alone here with your counterpart on these street stones?'

'I hardly seem yet,' returned Charles Darnay, 'to belong to this world again.'

'I don't wonder at it; it's not so long since you were pretty far advanced on your way to another. You speak faintly.'

'I begin to think I *am* faint.'

'Then why the devil don't you dine? I dined, myself, while those numskulls were deliberating which world you should belong to—this, or some other. Let me show you the nearest tavern to dine well at.'

Drawing his arm through his own, he took him to a tavern. Here, they were shown into a little room, where Charles Darnay was soon recruiting his strength with a good plain dinner and good wine: while Carton sat opposite to him at the same table, with his separate bottle of port before him, and his fully half-insolent manner upon him.

'Do you feel, yet, that you belong to this terrestrial scheme again, Mr. Darnay?'

'I am frightfully confused regarding time and place; but I am so far mended as to feel that.'

'It must be an immense satisfaction!'

He said it bitterly, and filled up his glass again: which was a large one.

Confused by the emotion of the day, and feeling his being there with this Double of coarse deportment, to be like a dream, Charles Darnay was at a loss how to answer; finally, answered not at all.

'Now your dinner is done,' Carton presently said, 'why don't you call a health, Mr. Darnay; why don't you give your toast?'

'What health? What toast?'

'Why, it's on the tip of your tongue. It ought to be, it must be, I'll swear it's there.'

'Miss Manette, then!'

'Miss Manette, then!'

Looking his companion full in the face while he drank the toast, Carton flung his glass over his shoulder against the wall, where it shivered to pieces; then, rang the bell, and ordered in another.

'That's a fair young lady to be pitied by and wept for by! How does it feel? Is it worth being tried for one's life, to be the object of such sympathy and compassion, Mr. Darnay?'

Darnay answered not a word.

'She was mightily pleased to have your message, when I gave it her. Not that she showed she was pleased, but I suppose she was.'

The allusion served as a timely reminder to Darnay that this disagreeable companion had, of his own free will, assisted him in the strait of the day. He turned the dialogue to that point, and thanked him for it.

'I neither want any thanks, nor merit any,' was the careless rejoiner. 'It was nothing to do, in the first place; and I don't know why I did it, in the second. Mr. Darnay, let me ask you a question.'

'Willingly, and a small return for your good offices.'

'Do you think I particularly like you?'

'Really, Mr. Carton,' returned the other, oddly disconcerted, 'I have not asked myself the question.'

'But ask yourself the question now.'

'You have acted as if you do; but I don't think you do.'

'*I* don't think I do,' said Carton. 'I begin to have a very good opinion of your understanding.'

'Nevertheless,' pursued Darnay, rising to ring the bell, 'there is nothing in that, I hope, to prevent my calling the reckoning, and our parting without ill-blood on either side.'

Carton rejoining, 'Nothing in life!' Darnay rang. 'Do you call the whole reckoning?' said Carton. On his answering in the affirmative, 'Then bring me another pint of this same wine, drawer, and come and wake me at ten.'

The bill being paid, Charles Darnay rose and wished him good-night. Without returning the wish, Carton rose too, with something of a threat of defiance in his manner, and said, 'A last word, Mr. Darnay: you think I am drunk?'

'I think you have been drinking, Mr. Carton.'

'Think? You know I have been drinking.'

'Since I must say so, I know it.'

'Then you shall likewise know why. I am a disappointed drudge, sir. I care for no man on earth, and no man on earth cares for me.'

'Much to be regretted. You might have used your talents better.'

'May be so, Mr. Darnay; may be not. Don't let your sober face elate you, however; you don't know what it may come to. Good-night!'

When he was left alone, this strange being took up a candle, went to a glass that hung against the wall, and surveyed himself minutely in it.

'Do you particularly like the man?' he muttered, at his own image; 'why should you particularly like a man who resembles you? There is nothing in you to like; you know that. Ah, confound you! What a change you have made in yourself! A good reason for taking to a man, that he shows you what you have fallen away from, and what you might have been! Change places with him, and would you have been looked at by those blue eyes as he was, and commiserated by that agitated face as he was? Come on, and have it out in plain words! You hate the fellow.'

He resorted to his pint of wine for consolation, drank it all in a few minutes, and fell asleep on his arms.

It had once been noted at the Bar, that while Mr. Stryver was a glib man, and an unscrupulous, and a ready, and a bold, he had not that faculty of extracting the essence from a heap of statements, which is among the most striking and necessary of the advocate's accomplishments. But a remarkable improvement came upon him as to this. The more business he got, the greater his power seemed to grow of getting at its pith and marrow; and however late at night he sat carousing with Sydney Carton, he always had his points at his fingers' ends in the morning.

Sydney Carton, idlest and most unpromising of men, was Stryver's great ally. Stryver never had a case in hand, anywhere, but Carton was there, with his hands in his pockets, staring at the ceiling of the court. At last, it began to get about, among such as were interested in the matter, that although Sydney Carton would never be a lion, he was an amazingly good jackal, and that he rendered service to Stryver in that humble capacity.

'Ten o'clock, sir,' said the man at the tavern, whom he had charged to wake him—'ten o'clock, sir.'

'*What's* the matter?'

'Ten o'clock, sir.'

'What do you mean? Ten o'clock at night?'

'Yes, sir. Your honour told me to call you.'

'Oh! I remember. Very well, very well.'

After a few dull efforts to get to sleep again, which the man dexterously combated by stirring the fire continuously, he got up, tossed his hat on, and walked out. He turned into the Temple, into Stryver's chambers. Stryver opened the door. He had his slippers on, and a loose bed-gown, and his throat was bare for his greater ease.

'You are a little late, Memory,' said Stryver.

'About the usual time; it may be a quarter of an hour later.'

They went into a dingy room lined with books and littered with papers, where there was a blazing fire. A kettle steamed upon the hob, and in the midst of the wreck of papers a table shone, with plenty of wine upon it, and brandy, and rum, and sugar, and lemons.

'You have had your bottle, I perceive, Sydney.'

'Two to-night, I think. I have been dining with the day's client; or seeing him dine—it's all one!'

'That was a rare point, Sydney, that you brought to bear upon the identification. How did you come by it? When did it strike you?'

'I thought he was rather a handsome fellow, and I thought I should have been much the same sort of fellow, if I had had any luck.'

Mr. Stryver laughed.

'You and your luck, Sydney! Get to work, get to work.'

Sullenly enough, the jackal loosened his dress, went into an adjoining room, and came back with a large jug of cold water, a basin, and a towel or two. Steeping the towels in the water, and partially wringing them out, he folded them on his head in a manner hideous to behold, sat down at the table, and said, 'Now I am ready!'

'Not much boiling down to be done to-night, Memory,' said Mr. Stryver, gaily, as he looked among his papers.

'How much?'

'Only two sets of them.'

'Give me the worst first.'

'There they are, Sydney. Fire away!'

The lion then composed himself on his back on a sofa on one side of the drinking-table, while the jackal sat at his own paper-bestrewn table proper, on the other side of it, with the bottles and glasses ready to his hand. Both resorted to the drinking-table without stint, but each in a different way; the lion for the most part reclining with his hands in his waistband, looking at the fire, or occasionally flirting with some lighter document; the jackal, with knitted brows and intent face, so deep in his task, that his eyes did not even follow the hand he stretched out for his glass.

At length the jackal had got together a compact repast for the lion, and proceeded to offer it to him. The lion took it with care and caution, made his selections from it, and his remarks upon it, and the jackal assisted both. When the repast was fully discussed, the lion put his hands in his waistband again, and lay down to meditate. The jackal then invigorated himself with a bumper for his throttle, and a fresh application to his head, and applied himself to the collection of a second meal; this was administered to the lion in the same manner, and was not disposed of until the clocks struck three in the morning.

'And now we have done, Sydney, fill a bumper of punch,' said Mr. Stryver.

The jackal removed the towels from his head, yawned, shivered, and complied.

'You were very sound, Sydney, in the matter of those crown witnesses to-day. Every question told.'

'I always am sound; am I not?'

'I don't gainsay it. What has roughened your temper? Put some punch to it and smooth it again.'

With a deprecatory grunt, the jackal again complied.

'The old Sydney Carton of old Shrewsbury School,' said Stryver, nodding his head over him as he reviewed him in the present, and the past, 'the old seesaw Sydney. Up one minute and down the next; now in spirits and now in despondency!'

'Ah!' returned the other, sighing: 'yes! The same Sydney, with the same luck. Even then, I did exercises for other boys, and seldom did my own.'

'And why not?'

'God knows. It was my way, I suppose. And now I'll have no more drink; I'll get to bed.'

---

6 · HUNDREDS OF PEOPLE

THE quiet lodgings of Doctor Manette were in a quiet street-corner not far from Soho-square. On the afternoon of a certain fine Sunday, four months after the trial for treason, Mr. Jarvis Lorry walked along the sunny streets to dine with the Doctor. After several relapses into business-absorption, Mr. Lorry had become the Doctor's friend, and the quiet street-corner was the sunny part of his life.

The summer light struck into the corner brilliantly in the earlier part of the day; but, when the streets grew hot, the corner was in shadow. It was a cool spot, staid but cheerful, a wonderful place for echoes, and a very harbour from the raging streets.

Doctor Manette received such patients here as his old reputation, and its revival in the floating whispers of his story, brought him. His scientific knowledge, and his vigilance and skill in conducting ingenious experiments, brought him otherwise into moderate request, and he earned as much as he wanted.

These things were within Mr. Jarvis Lorry's knowledge,

when he rang the door-bell of the tranquil house in the corner, on the fine Sunday afternoon.

'Doctor Manette at home?'

Expected home.

'Miss Lucie at home?'

Expected home.

'Miss Pross at home?'

Possibly at home.

'As I am at home myself,' said Mr. Lorry, 'I'll go upstairs.'

There were three rooms on a floor, and, the doors by which they communicated being put open that the air might pass freely through them all, Mr. Lorry, smilingly observant of the delicate feminine touches which he detected all around him, walked from one to another. The first was the best room, and in it were Lucie's birds, and flowers, and books, and desk, and work-table, and box of water-colours; the second was the Doctor's consulting-room, used also as the dining-room; the third, changingly speckled by the rustle of the plane-tree in the yard, was the Doctor's bedroom, and there, in a corner, stood the disused shoemaker's bench and tray of tools, much as it had stood on the fifth floor of the dismal house by the wine-shop, in the suburb of Saint Antoine in Paris.

'I wonder,' said Mr. Lorry, pausing in his looking about, 'that he keeps that reminder of his sufferings about him!'

'And why wonder at that?' was the abrupt inquiry that made him start.

It proceeded from Miss Pross, the wild red woman, strong of hand, whose acquaintance he had first made at the Royal George Hotel at Dover, and had since improved.

'I should have thought——' Mr. Lorry began.

'Pooh! You'd have thought!' said Miss Pross; and Mr. Lorry left off.

'How do you do?' inquired that lady then—sharply, and yet as if to express that she bore him no malice.

'I am pretty well, I thank you,' answered Mr. Lorry, with meekness; 'how are you?'

'Nothing to boast of,' said Miss Pross.

'Indeed?'

'Ah! indeed!' said Miss Pross. 'I am very much put out about my Ladybird.'

'Indeed?'

'I don't want dozens of people who are not at all worthy of Ladybird, to come here looking after her,' said Miss Pross.

'*Do* dozens come for that purpose?'

'Hundreds,' said Miss Pross.

It was characteristic of this lady (as of some other people before her time and since) that whenever her original proposition was questioned, she exaggerated it.

'Dear me!' said Mr. Lorry, as the safest remark he could think of.

Mr. Lorry knew Miss Pross to be very jealous, but he also knew her by this time to be, beneath the surface of her eccentricity, one of those unselfish creatures—found only among women—who will, for pure love and admiration, bind themselves willing slaves, to youth when they have lost it, to beauty that they never had.

'As we happen to be alone for the moment, and are both people of business,' he said, when they had got back to the drawing-room and had sat down there in friendly relations, 'let me ask you—does the Doctor, in talking with Lucie, ever refer to the shoemaking time, yet?'

'Never.'

'And yet keeps that bench and those tools beside him?'

'Ah!' returned Miss Pross, shaking her head. 'But I don't say he don't refer to it within himself.'

'Do you believe that he thinks of it much?'

'I do,' said Miss Pross.

'Do you imagine——' Mr. Lorry had begun, when Miss Pross took him up short with:

'Never imagine anything. Have no imagination at all.'

'I stand corrected; do you suppose—you go so far as to suppose, sometimes?'

'Now and then,' said Miss Pross.

'Do you suppose,' Mr. Lorry went on, with a laughing twinkle in his bright eye, as it looked kindly at her, 'that Doctor Manette has any theory of his own, preserved through all those years, relative to the cause of his being so oppressed; perhaps, even to the name of his oppressor?'

'I don't suppose anything about it but what Ladybird tells me.'

'And that is——?'

'That she thinks he has.'

'Now don't be angry at my asking all these questions; because I am a mere dull man of business. Is it not remarkable that Doctor Manette, unquestionably innocent of any crime as we are all well assured he is, should never touch upon that question? I will not say with me, though he had business relations with me many years ago, and we are now intimate; I will say with the fair daughter to whom he is so devotedly attached, and who is so devotedly attached to him?'

'Well! To the best of my understanding,' said Miss Pross, 'he is afraid of the whole subject.'

'Afraid?'

'It's plain enough, I should think, why he may be. It's a dreadful remembrance. Besides that, his loss of himself grew out of it. Not knowing how he lost himself, or how he recovered himself, he may never feel certain of not losing himself again.'

It was a profounder remark than Mr. Lorry had looked for. 'True,' said he, 'and fearful to reflect upon. Yet, a doubt lurks in my mind, Miss Pross, whether it is good for Doctor Manette to have that suppression always shut up within him. Indeed, it is this doubt and the uneasiness it sometimes causes me that has led me to our present confidence.'

'Can't be helped,' said Miss Pross, shaking her head. 'Touch that string, and he instantly changes for the worse. Better leave it alone. Sometimes, he gets up in the dead of night, and will be heard, by us overhead there, walking up and down, walking up and down, in his room. Ladybird has learnt to know then that his mind is walking up and down, walking up and down, in his old prison. She hurries to him, and they go on together, walking up and down, walking up and down, until he is composed. But he never says a word of the true reason of his restlessness, to her, and she finds it best not to hint at it to him. In silence they go walking up and down together, walking up and down together, till her love and company have brought him to himself.'

Notwithstanding Miss Pross's denial of her own imagination, there was a perception of the pain of being monotonously haunted by one sad idea, in her repetition of the phrase, walking up and down, which testified to her possessing such a thing.

The corner has been mentioned as a wonderful corner for

echoes; it had begun to echo so resoundingly to the tread of coming feet, that it seemed as though the very mention of that weary pacing to and fro had set it going.

'Here they are!' said Miss Pross, rising to break up the conference; 'and now we shall have hundreds of people pretty soon!'

Miss Pross was a pleasant sight, though wild, and red, and grim, taking off her darling's bonnet when she came upstairs. Her darling was a pleasant sight too, embracing her and thanking her. The Doctor was a pleasant sight too, looking on at them, and telling Miss Pross how she spoilt Lucie, in accents and with eyes that had as much spoiling in them as Miss Pross had. Mr. Lorry was a pleasant sight too, beaming at all this and thanking his bachelor stars for having lighted him in his declining years to a home. But, no Hundreds of people came to see the sights, and Mr. Lorry looked in vain for the fulfilment of Miss Pross's prediction.

Dinner-time, and still no Hundreds of people. It was an oppressive day, and, after dinner, Lucie proposed that the wine should be carried out under the plane-tree, and they should sit there in the air.

Still, the Hundreds of people did not present themselves. Mr. Darnay presented himself while they were sitting under the plane-tree, but he was only One.

Doctor Manette received him kindly, and so did Lucie. But, Miss Pross suddenly became afflicted with a twitching in the head and body, and retired into the house. She was not unfrequently the victim of this disorder, and she called it, in familiar conversation, 'a fit of the jerks'.

The Doctor was in his best condition, and looked specially young. The resemblance between him and Lucie was very strong at such times, and as they sat side by side, she leaning on his shoulder, and he resting his arm on the back of her chair, it was very agreeable to trace the likeness.

Tea-time, and Miss Pross making tea, with another fit of the jerks upon her, and yet no Hundreds of people. Mr. Carton had lounged in, but he made only Two.

The night was so very sultry, that although they sat with doors and windows open, they were overpowered by heat. When the tea-table was done with, they all moved to one of the windows, and looked out into the heavy twilight. Lucie sat by her father; Darnay sat beside her; Carton leaned against a window.

'The rain-drops are falling, large, heavy, and few,' said Doctor Manette. 'It comes slowly.'

'It comes surely,' said Carton.

They spoke low, as people watching and waiting mostly do; as people in a dark room, watching and waiting for lightning, always do.

There was a great hurry in the streets, of people speeding away to get shelter before the storm broke; the wonderful corner for echoes resounded with the echoes of footsteps coming and going, yet not a footstep was there.

'A multitude of people, and yet a solitude!' said Darnay, when they had listened for a while.

'Is it not impressive, Mr. Darnay?' asked Lucie. 'Sometimes I have sat here of an evening, until I have fancied—until I have made the echoes out to be the echoes of all the footsteps that are coming by-and-by into our lives.'

'There is a great crowd coming one day into our lives, if that be so,' Sydney Carton struck in, in his moody way.

The footsteps were incessant, and the hurry of them became more and more rapid. The corner echoed and re-echoed with the tread of feet; some, as it seemed, under the windows; some, as it seemed, in the room; some coming, some going, and not one within sight.

'Are all these footsteps destined to come to all of us, Miss Manette, or are we to divide them among us?'

'I don't know, Mr. Darnay; a foolish fancy, but I have imagined them the footsteps of the people who are to come into my life, and my father's.'

'I take them into mine!' said Carton. 'There is a great crowd bearing down upon us, Miss Manette, and I see them —by the lightning.' He added the last words, after there had been a vivid flash which had shown him lounging in the window.

'And I hear them!' he added again, after a peal of thunder. 'Here they come, fast, fierce, and furious!'

It was the rush and roar of rain that he typified, and it stopped him, for no voice could be heard in it. A memorable storm of thunder and lightning broke with that sweep of water, and there was not a moment's interval in crash, and fire, and rain, until after the moon rose at midnight.

The great bell of Saint Paul's was striking One in the cleared air, when Mr. Lorry, escorted by Jerry, high-booted and bearing a lantern, set forth on his return-passage to Clerkenwell. There were solitary patches of road on the way between Soho and Clerkenwell, and Mr. Lorry, mindful of footpads, always retained Jerry for this service: though it was usually performed a good two hours earlier.

'What a night it has been! Good-night, Mr. Carton,' said the man of business, as their ways parted. 'Good-night, Mr. Darnay. Shall we ever see such a night again, together?'

Perhaps. Perhaps, see the great crowd of people with its rush and roar, bearing down upon them, too.

7 · MONSIEUR THE MARQUIS

WITH a wild rattle and clatter, and an inhuman abandonment of consideration not easy to be understood in these days, a carriage dashed through the streets of Paris and swept round corners, with women screaming before it, and men clutching each other and clutching children out of its way. At last, swooping at a street corner by a fountain, one of its wheels came to a sickening little jolt, and there was a loud cry from a number of voices, and the horses reared and plunged.

But for the latter inconvenience, the carriage probably would not have stopped; carriages were often known to drive on, and leave their wounded behind, and why not? But the frightened valet had got down in a hurry, and there were twenty hands at the horses' bridles.

'What has gone wrong?' said Monsieur, calmly looking out.

A tall man in a nightcap had caught up a bundle, and had laid it on the basement of the fountain, and was down in the mud and wet, howling over it like a wild animal.

'Pardon, Monsieur the Marquis!' said a ragged and submissive man, 'it is a child.'

'Why does he make that abominable noise? Is it his child?'

'Excuse me, Monsieur the Marquis—it is a pity—yes.'

The fountain was a little removed; for the street opened, where it was, into a space some ten or twelve yards square. As the tall man suddenly got up from the ground, and came running at the carriage, Monsieur the Marquis clapped his hand for an instant on his sword-hilt.

'Killed!' shrieked the man, in wild desperation, extending

both arms at their length above his head, and staring at him. 'Dead!'

The people closed round, and looked at Monsieur the Marquis. There was nothing revealed by the many eyes that looked at him but watchfulness and eagerness; there was no visible menacing or anger. Monsieur the Marquis ran his eyes over them all, as if they had been mere rats come out of their holes.

He took out his purse.

'It is extraordinary to me,' said he, 'that you people cannot take care of yourselves and your children. One or the other of you is for ever in the way. How do I know what injury you have done my horses? See! Give him that.'

He threw out a gold coin for the valet to pick up, and all the heads craned forward that all the eyes might look down at it as it fell. The tall man called out again with a most unearthly cry, 'Dead!'

He was arrested by the quick arrival of another man, for whom the rest made way. On seeing him, the miserable creature fell upon his shoulder, sobbing and crying, and pointing to the fountain, where some women were stooping over the motionless bundle, and moving gently about it. They were as silent, however, as the men.

'I know all, I know all,' said the last comer. 'Be a brave man, my Gaspard! It is better for the poor little plaything to die so, than to live.'

'You are a philosopher, you there,' said the Marquis, smiling. 'How do they call you?'

'They call me Defarge.'

'Of what trade?'

'Monsieur the Marquis, vendor of wine.'

'Pick up that, philosopher and vendor of wine,' said the

Marquis, throwing him another gold coin, 'and spend it as you will. The horses there; are they right?'

Without deigning to look at the assemblage a second time, Monsieur the Marquis leaned back in his seat, and was just being driven away with the air of a gentleman who had accidentally broken some common thing, and had paid for it, and could afford to pay for it; when his ease was suddenly disturbed by a coin flying into his carriage, and ringing on its floor.

'Hold!' said Monsieur the Marquis. 'Hold the horses! Who threw that?'

He looked to the spot where Defarge the vendor of wine had stood, a moment before; but the wretched father was grovelling on his face on the pavement in that spot, and the figure that stood beside him was the figure of a dark stout woman, knitting.

'You dogs!' said the Marquis, but smoothly, and with an unchanged front. 'If I knew which rascal threw at the carriage, he should be crushed under the wheels.'

So cowed was their condition, and so long and hard their experience of what such a man could do to them, that not a voice, or a hand, or even an eye was raised. Among the men, not one. But the woman who stood knitting looked up steadily, and looked the Marquis in the face. It was not for his dignity to notice it; his contemptuous eyes passed over her, and over all the other rats; and he leaned back in his seat again, and gave the word 'Go on!'

A beautiful landscape with the corn bright in it, but not abundant. Patches of poor rye where corn should have been, patches of poor peas and beans, patches of most coarse vegetable substitutes for wheat. Monsieur the Marquis in his travelling carriage (which might have been lighter), conducted by four post-horses and two postilions, fagged up a steep hill.

The sunset struck so brilliantly into the travelling carriage when it gained the hill-top, that its occupant was steeped in crimson. 'It will die out,' said Monsieur the Marquis. In effect, the sun was so low that it dipped at the moment. When the heavy drag had been adjusted to the wheel, and the carriage slid down hill, in a cloud of dust, the red glow departed quickly; the sun and the Marquis going down together, there was no glow left when the drag was taken off.

But, there remained a broken country, bold and open, a little village at the bottom of the hill, a broad sweep and rise beyond it, a church-tower, a windmill, a forest for the chase, and a crag with a fortress on it used as a prison. Round upon all these darkening objects as the night drew on, the Marquis looked, with the air of one who was coming near home.

The village had its one poor street, with its poor tavern, poor stable-yard for relay of post-horses, poor fountain. It had its poor people too. All its people were poor, and many of them were sitting at their doors, shredding spare onions and the like for supper, while many were at the fountain, washing leaves, and grasses, and any such small yieldings of the earth that could be eaten. Expressive signs of what made them poor, were not wanting; the tax for the state, the tax for the church, the tax for the lord, tax local and tax general, were to be paid here and to be paid there, according to solemn inscription in the little village, until the wonder was, that there was any village left unswallowed.

Monsieur the Marquis drew up in his travelling carriage at the posting-house gate. It was hard by the fountain, and the peasants suspended their operations to look at him.

Monsieur the Marquis cast his eyes over the submissive faces that drooped before him, when a grizzled mender of the roads joined the group.

'Bring me hither that fellow!' said the Marquis to the courier.

The fellow was brought, cap in hand, and the other fellows closed round to look and listen.

'I passed you on the road?'

'Monseigneur, it is true. I had the honour of being passed on the road.'

'What did you look at, so fixedly?'

'Monseigneur, I looked at the man.'

He stooped a little, and with his tattered blue cap pointed under the carriage. All his fellows stooped to looked under the carriage.

'What man, pig? And why look there?'

'Pardon, Monseigneur; he swung by the chain of the shoe—the drag.'

'Who?' demanded the traveller.

'Monseigneur, the man.'

'May the Devil carry away these idiots! How do you call the man? You know all the men of this part of the country. Who was he?'

'Your clemency, Monseigneur! He was not of this part of the country. Of all the days of my life, I never saw him.'

'Swinging by the chain? To be suffocated?'

'With your gracious permission, that was the wonder of it, Monseigneur. His head hanging over—like this!'

He turned himself sideways to the carriage, and leaned back, with his face thrown up to the sky, and his head hanging down; then recovered himself, fumbled with his cap, and made a bow.

'What was he like?'

'Monseigneur, he was whiter than the miller. All covered with dust, white as a spectre, tall as a spectre!'

All eyes looked at Monsieur the Marquis. Perhaps, to observe whether he had any spectre on his conscience.

'Truly, you did well,' said the Marquis 'to see a thief accompanying my carriage, and not open that great mouth of yours. Bah! Put him aside, Monsieur Gabelle!'

Monsieur Gabelle was the Postmaster, and some other taxing functionary united; he had come out with great obsequiousness to assist at this examination, and had held the examined by his arm in an official manner.

'Bah! Go aside!' said Monsieur Gabelle.

'Lay hands on this stranger if he seeks to lodge in your village to-night, and be sure that his business is honest, Gabelle.'

'Monseigneur, I am flattered to devote myself to your orders.'

'Did he run away, fellow?—where is that Accursed?'

The accursed was already under the carriage with some half-dozen particular friends, pointing out the chain with his blue cap. Some half-dozen other particular friends promptly hauled him out, and presented him breathless to Monsieur the Marquis.

'Did the man run away, Dolt, when we stopped for the drag?'

'Monseigneur, he precipitated himself over the hillside, head first, as a person plunges into the river.'

'See to it, Gabelle. Go on!'

The burst with which the carriage started out of the village and up the rise beyond, was soon checked by the steepness of the hill. Gradually, it subsided to a foot pace, swinging and lumbering upward among the many sweet scents of a summer night. The sweet scents of the summer night rose all around, on the dusty, ragged, and toil-worn group at the fountain to whom the mender of roads, with the aid of the blue cap without which he was nothing, still enlarged upon his man like a spectre, as long as they could bear it. By degrees, as they could bear no more, they dropped off one by one, and lights twinkled in little casements.

The shadow of a large high-roofed house, and of many overhanging trees, was upon Monsieur the Marquis by that time; and the shadow was exchanged for the light of a flambeau, as his carriage stopped, and the great door of his château was opened to him.

'Monsieur Charles, whom I expect; is he arrived from England?'

'Monseigneur, not yet.'

Up the broad flight of shallow steps, Monsieur the Marquis, flambeau-preceded, went from his carriage. The great door clanged behind him, and Monsieur the Marquis crossed a hall grim with certain old boar-spears, swords, and knives of the chase; grimmer with certain heavy riding-rods and riding-whips, of which many a peasant had felt the weight when his lord was angry.

Avoiding the larger rooms, which were dark and made fast for the night, Monsieur the Marquis, with his flambeau-bearer going on before, went up the staircase to a door in a corridor. This thrown open, admitted him to his own private apartment of three rooms: his bed-chamber and two others. A supper-table was laid for two in the third of the rooms.

'My nephew,' said the Marquis, glancing at the supper preparations; 'they said he was not arrived.'

Nor was he; but, he had been expected with Monseigneur.

'Ah! Leave the table as it is. I shall be ready in a quarter of an hour.'

In a quarter of an hour Monseigneur was ready, and sat down alone to his sumptuous and choice supper. His chair was opposite to the window, and he had taken his soup, and was raising his glass of wine to his lips, when he put it down.

'What is that?' he calmly asked, looking with attention at the window.

'Monseigneur? That?'

'Outside the blinds. Open the blinds.'

It was done.

'Well?'

'Monseigneur, it is nothing. The trees and the night are all that are here.'

The servant who spoke, had thrown the blinds wide, had looked out into the vacant darkness, and stood, with that blank behind him, looking round for instructions.

'Good,' said the imperturbable master. 'Close them again.'

That was done too, and the Marquis went on with his supper. He was half-way through it, when he again stopped with his glass in his hand, hearing the sound of wheels. It came on briskly, and came up to the front of the château.

'Ask who is arrived.'

It was the nephew of Monseigneur. He had been some few leagues behind Monseigneur. He had heard of Monseigneur, at the posting-houses, as being before him.

He was to be told (said Monseigneur) that supper awaited him then and there, and that he was prayed to come to it. In a little while he came. He had been known in England as Charles Darnay.

Monseigneur received him in a courtly manner, but they did not shake hands.

'You left Paris, yesterday, sir?' he said to Monseigneur, as he took his seat at table.

'Yesterday. And you?'

'I come direct.'

'From London?'

'Yes.'

'You have been a long time coming,' said the Marquis, with a smile.

'On the contrary; I come direct.'

'Pardon me! I mean, not a long time on the journey; a long time intending the journey.'

'I have been detained by'—the nephew stopped a moment in his answer—'various business.'

'Without doubt,' said the polished uncle.

So long as a servant was present, no other words passed between them. When coffee had been served and they were alone together, the nephew, looking at the uncle and meeting the eyes of the face that was like a fine mask, opened a conversation.

'Sir,' said the nephew, 'we have done wrong, and are reaping the fruits of wrong.'

'*We* have done wrong?' repeated the Marquis, with an inquiring smile, and delicately pointing, first to his nephew, then to himself.

'Our family. Even in my father's time, we did a world of wrong, injuring every human creature who came between us and our pleasure, whatever it was. Why need I speak of my father's time, when it is equally yours? Can I separate my father's twin-brother, joint inheritor, and next successor, from himself?'

'Death has done that!' said the Marquis.

'And has left me,' answered the nephew, 'bound to a

system that is frightful to me, responsible for it, but powerless in it; seeking to execute the last request of my dear mother's lips, and obey the last look of my dear mother's eyes, which implored me to have mercy and to redress; and tortured by seeking assistance and power in vain.'

'Seeking them from me, my nephew,' said the Marquis, touching him on the breast with his forefinger—they were now standing by the hearth—'you will for ever seek them in vain, be assured.

'Better to be a rational creature,' he added then, 'and accept your natural destiny. But you are lost, Monsieur Charles, I see.'

'This property and France are lost to me,' said the nephew, sadly; 'I renounce them.'

'Are they both yours to renounce? France may be, but is the property? It is scarcely worth mentioning; but, is it yet?'

'I had no intention, in the words I used, to claim it yet. If it passed to me from you, to-morrow——'

'Which I have the vanity to hope is not probable.'

'—or twenty years hence——'

'You do me too much honour,' said the Marquis; 'still, I prefer that supposition.'

'—I would abandon it, and live otherwise and elsewhere. It is little to relinquish. What is it but a wilderness of misery and ruin?'

'Hah!' said the Marquis, glancing round the luxurious room.

'To the eye it is fair enough, here; but seen in its integrity, under the sky, and by the daylight, it is a crumbling tower of waste, mismanagement, extortion, debt, mortgage, oppression, hunger, nakedness, and suffering.'

'Hah!' said the Marquis again, in a well-satisfied manner.

'If it ever becomes mine, it shall be put into some hands better qualified to free it slowly (if such a thing is possible) from the weight that drags it down, so that the miserable people who cannot leave it and who have been long wrung to the last point of endurance, may, in another generation, suffer less; but it is not for me. There is a curse on it, and on all this land.'

'And you?' said the uncle. 'Forgive my curiosity; how do you, under your new philosophy, intend to live?'

'I must do, to live, what others of my countrymen, even with nobility at their backs, may have to do some day—work.'

The thin straight lines of the setting of the eyes, and the thin straight lips, curved with a sarcasm that looked handsomely diabolic.

'Yes,' said the Marquis. 'So commences the new philosophy! You are fatigued. Good-night!'

Dead darkness lay on all the landscape, dead darkness added its own hush to the hushing dust on all the roads. In the village, taxers and taxed were fast asleep. Dreaming, perhaps, of banquets, as the starved usually do, and of ease and rest, as the driven slave and the yoked ox may, its lean inhabitants slept soundly, and were fed and free.

The fountain in the village flowed unseen and unheard through three dark hours. Then the grey water began to be ghostly in the light. Lighter and lighter, until at last the sun touched the tops of the still trees, and poured its radiance over the hill. The carol of the birds was loud and high, and, on the sill of the great window of the bedchamber of Monsieur the Marquis, one little bird sang its sweetest song with all its might.

Now, the sun was full up, and movement began in the village. Casement windows opened, crazy doors were unbarred, and people came forth shivering—chilled, as yet, by the new sweet air. Then began the rarely lightened toil of the day among the village population. Some, to the fountain; some, to the fields; men and women here, to dig and delve; men and women there, to see to the poor live-stock, and lead the bony cows out, to such pasture as could be found by the roadside.

The château awoke later, as became its quality, but awoke gradually and surely. Doors and windows were thrown open, horses in their stables looked round over their shoulders at the light and freshness pouring in at doorways, leaves sparkled and rustled at iron-grated windows, dogs pulled hard at their chains, and reared impatient to be loosed.

All these trivial incidents belonged to the routine of life, and the return of morning. Surely, not so the ringing of the great bell of the château, nor the running up and down the stairs; nor the hurried figures on the terrace; nor the booting and tramping here and there and everywhere, nor the quick saddling of horses and riding away?

The Marquis was still in bed.

Driven home into the heart of his dead body was a knife. Round its hilt was a frill of paper on which was scrawled:

'Drive him fast to his tomb. This from JACQUES.'

---

8 · TWO PROMISES

MORE months, to the number of twelve, had come and gone, and Mr. Charles Darnay was established in England as a higher teacher of the French language who was conversant with French literature. As a tutor, whose attainments made the student's way unusually pleasant and profitable, and as an elegant translator who brought something to his work besides mere dictionary knowledge, young Mr. Darnay soon became known and encouraged. He was well acquainted, moreover, with the circumstances of his country, and those were of ever-growing interest. So, with great perseverance and untiring industry, he prospered.

Now, from the days when it was always summer in Eden, to these days when it is mostly winter in fallen latitudes, the world of a man has invariably gone one way—Charles Darnay's way—the way of the love of a woman.

He had loved Lucie Manette from the hour of his danger. He had never heard a sound so sweet and dear as the sound of her compassionate voice; he had never seen a face so tenderly beautiful, as hers when it was confronted with his own on the edge of the grave that had been dug for him. But, he had not yet spoken to her on the subject; the assassination at the deserted château far away beyond the heaving water and the long, long, dusty roads had been done a year, and he had never yet, by so much as a single spoken word, disclosed to her the state of his heart.

That he had his reasons for this, he knew full well. It was again a summer day when, lately arrived in London from his work at Cambridge, he turned into the quiet corner in Soho, bent on seeking an opportunity of opening his mind to Doctor Manette. It was the close of the summer day, and he knew Lucie to be out with Miss Pross.

He found the Doctor reading in his arm-chair at a window. He was now a very energetic man indeed, with great firmness of purpose, strength of resolution, and vigour of action. In his recovered energy he was sometimes a little fitful and sudden, as he had at first been in the exercise of his other recovered faculties; but, this had never been frequently observable, and had grown more and more rare. To him, now entered Charles Darnay, at sight of whom he laid aside his book and held out his hand.

'Charles Darnay! I rejoice to see you. We have been counting on your return these three or four days past. Mr. Stryver and Sydney Carton were both here yesterday, and both made you out to be more than due.'

'I am obliged to them for their interest in the matter,' he answered, a little coldly as to them, though very warmly as to the Doctor. 'Miss Manette——'

'Is well,' said the Doctor, as he stopped short, 'and your return will delight us all. She has gone out on some household matters, but will soon be home.'

'Doctor Manette, I knew she was from home. I took the opportunity of her being from home, to beg to speak to you.'

There was a blank silence.

'Yes?' said the Doctor, with evident constraint. 'Bring your chair here, and speak on.'

He complied as to the chair, but appeared to find the speaking on less easy.

'I have had the happiness, Doctor Manette, of being so intimate here,' so he at length began, 'for some year and a half, that I hope the topic on which I am about to touch may not——'

He was stayed by the Doctor's putting out his hand to stop him. When he had kept it so a little while, he said, drawing it back:

'Is Lucie the topic?'

'She is.'

'It is hard for me to speak of her at any time. It is very

hard for me to hear her spoken of in that tone of yours, Charles Darnay.'

'It is a tone of fervent admiration, true homage, and deep love, Doctor Manette!' he said deferentially.

There was another blank silence before her father rejoined:

'I believe it. I do you justice; I believe it.'

His constraint was so manifest that Charles Darnay hesitated.

'Shall I go on, sir?'

Another blank.

'Yes, go on.'

At last Darnay brought himself to declare his love for Lucie and to beg the Doctor to believe in its sincerity and purity. Her father appeared to consider before he answered:

'I believe your object to be, purely and truthfully, as you have stated it. I believe your intention is to perpetuate, and not to weaken, the ties between me and my other and far dearer self. If she should ever tell me that you are essential to her perfect happiness, I will give her to you. If there were —Charles Darnay, if there were——'

The young man had taken his hand gratefully; their hands were joined as the Doctor spoke:

'—any fancies, any reasons, any apprehensions, anything whatsoever, new or old, against the man she really loved— the direct responsibility thereof not lying on his head—they should all be obliterated for her sake. She is everything to me; more to me than suffering, more to me than wrong, more to me—— Well! This is idle talk.'

So strange was the way in which he faded into silence, and so strange his fixed look when he had ceased to speak, that Darnay felt his own hand turn cold in the hand that slowly released and dropped it.

Somewhat at a loss, Darnay persevered:

'Your confidence in me ought to be returned with full confidence on my part. My present name, though but slightly changed from my mother's, is not, as you will remember, my own. I wish to tell you what that is, and why I am in England.'

'Stop!' said the Doctor of Beauvais.

'I wish it, that I may the better deserve your confidence, and have no secret from you.'

'Stop!'

For an instant, the Doctor even had his two hands at his ears.

'Tell me when I ask you, not now. If your suit should prosper, if Lucie should love you, you shall tell me on your marriage morning. Do you promise?'

'Willingly.'

'Give me your hand. She will be home directly, and it is better she should not see us together to-night. Go! God bless you!'

It was dark when Charles Darnay left him, and it was an hour later and darker when Lucie came home; she hurried into the room alone—for Miss Pross had gone straight upstairs—and was surprised to find his reading-chair empty.

'My father!' she called to him. 'Father dear!'

Nothing was said in answer, but she heard a low hammering sound in his bedroom. Passing lightly across the intermediate room, she looked in at his door and came running back frightened, crying to herself, with her blood all chilled, 'What shall I do! What shall I do!'

Her uncertainty lasted but a moment; she hurried back, and tapped at his door, and softly called to him. The noise ceased at the sound of her voice, and he presently came out to her, and they walked up and down together for a long time.

She came down from her bed, to look at him in his sleep that night. He slept heavily, and his tray of shoe-making tools, and his old unfinished work, were all as usual.

If Sydney Carton ever shone anywhere, he certainly never shone in the house of Dr. Manette. He had been there often, during a whole year, and had always been the same moody and morose lounger there. When he cared to talk, he talked well; but, the cloud of caring for nothing, which overshadowed him with such a fatal darkness, was very rarely pierced by the light within him.

On a day in August, he was shown up-stairs, and found Lucie at her work, alone. She had never been quite at her ease with him, and received him with some little embarrassment as he seated himself near her table. But, looking up at his face in the interchange of the first few commonplaces, she observed a change in it.

'I fear you are not well, Mr. Carton!'

'No. But the life I lead, Miss Manette, is not conducive to health. What is to be expected of, or by, such profligates?'

'Is it not—forgive me; I have begun the question on my lips—a pity to live no better life?'

'God knows it is a shame!'

'Then why not change it?'

Looking gently at him again, she was surprised and saddened to see that there were tears in his eyes. There were tears in his voice too, as he answered:

'It is too late for that. I shall never be better than I am. I shall sink lower, and be worse.'

She had never seen him softened, and was much distressed. He knew her to be so, without looking at her, and said:

'Pray forgive me, Miss Manette. I break down before the knowledge of what I want to say to you. Will you hear me?'

'If it will do you any good, Mr. Carton, if it would make you happier, it would make me very glad!'

'God bless you for your sweet compassion! Don't be afraid to hear me. Don't shrink from anything I say. I am like one who died young. All my life might have been.'

'No, Mr. Carton. I am sure that the best part of it might still be; I am sure that you might be much, much worthier of yourself.'

'Say of you, Miss Manette, and although I know better—although in my own wretched heart I know better—I shall never forget it!'

She was pale and trembling. He came to her relief with a fixed despair of himself which made the interview unlike any other that could have been holden.

'If it had been possible, Miss Manette, that you could have returned the love of the man you see before you—self-flung away, wasted, drunken, poor creature of misuse as you know him to be—he would have been conscious this day and hour, in spite of his happiness, that he would bring you to misery, bring you to sorrow and repentance, blight you, disgrace you, pull you down with him. I know very well that you can have no tenderness for me; I ask for none; I am even thankful that it cannot be.'

'Without it, can I not save you, Mr. Carton? Can I not recall you—forgive me again!—to a better course?'

He shook his head.

'If you will hear me through a very little more, all you can ever do for me is done. I wish you to know that you have been the last dream of my soul. In my degradation I have not been so degraded but that the sight of you with your father, and of this home made such a home by you, has stirred old shadows that I thought had died out of me. I have had unformed ideas of striving afresh, beginning anew, shaking off sloth and sensuality, and fighting out the abandoned fight. A dream, all a dream, but I wish you to know that you inspired it.'

'Will nothing of it remain? O Mr. Carton, think again! Try again!'

'No, Miss Manette, an hour or two hence, and the low companions and low habits that I scorn but yield to, will render me less worth such tears as those, than any wretch who creeps along the streets. Be comforted! But, within myself, I shall always be, towards you, what I am now, though outwardly I shall be what you have heretofore seen me. The last supplication but one I make to you, is, that you will believe this of me.'

'I will, Mr. Carton.'

'My last supplication of all, is this; and with it, I will relieve you of a visitor between whom and you there is an impassable space. It is useless to say it, I know, but it rises out of my soul. For you, and for any dear to you, I would do anything. If my career were of that better kind that there was any opportunity or capacity of sacrifice in it, I would embrace any sacrifice for you and for those dear to you. Try to hold me in your mind, at some quiet times, as ardent and sincere in this one thing. The time will come, the time will not be long in coming, when new ties will be formed about you—ties that will bind you yet more tenderly and strongly to the home you so adorn—the dearest ties that will ever grace and gladden you. O Miss Manette, when you see your own bright beauty springing up anew at your feet, think now and then that there is a man who would give his life, to keep a life you love beside you!'

He said, 'Farewell!' and a last 'God bless you!' and left her.

---

9 · KNITTING

THERE had been earlier drinking than usual in the wine-shop of Monsieur Defarge. As early as six o'clock in the morning, sallow faces peeping through its barred windows had seen other faces within, bending over measures of wine. This had been the third morning in succession, on which there had been early drinking at the wine-shop of Monsieur Defarge.

In spite of the unusual flow of company, the master of the wine-shop was not visible. He was not missed; for nobody who crossed the threshold looked for him, nobody asked for him, nobody wondered to see only Madame Defarge in her seat, presiding over the distribution of wine.

It was high noontide, when two dusty men passed through the streets and under the swinging lamps: of whom, one was Monsieur Defarge: the other a mender of roads in a blue cap. No one had followed them, and no man spoke when they entered the wine-shop, though the eyes of every man there were turned upon them.

'Good-day, gentlemen!' said Monsieur Defarge.

There was an answering chorus.

'It is bad weather, gentlemen,' said Defarge, shaking his head.

Upon which, every man looked at his neighbour, and then all cast down their eyes and sat silent. Except one man, who got up and went out.

'My wife,' said Defarge aloud, addressing Madame Defarge: 'I have travelled certain leagues with this good mender of roads, called Jacques. I met him—by accident—a day and a half's journey out of Paris. He is a good child, this mender of roads, called Jacques. Give him to drink, my wife!'

A second man got up and went out. Madame Defarge set wine before the mender of roads called Jacques, who doffed his blue cap to the company, and drank. In the breast of his blouse he carried some coarse dark bread; he ate of this between whiles, and sat munching and drinking near Madame Defarge's counter. A third man got up and went out.

Defarge stood waiting until the countryman had made his breakfast. He looked at no one present, and no one now looked at him; not even Madame Defarge, who had taken up her knitting, and was at work.

'Have you finished your repast, friend?' he asked, in due season.

'Yes, thank you.'

'Come, then! You shall see the apartment that I told you you could occupy. It will suit you to a marvel.'

Out of the wine-shop into a court-yard, up a steep staircase, into a garret,—formerly the garret where a white-haired man sat on a low bench, stooping forward and very busy, making shoes.

No white-haired man was there now; but, the three men were there who had gone out of the wine-shop singly. And between them and the white-haired man afar off, was the one small link, that they had once looked in at him through the chinks in the wall.

Defarge closed the door carefully, and spoke in a subdued voice:

'Jacques One, Jacques Two, Jacques Three! This is the witness encountered by appointment, by me, Jacques Four. He will tell you all. Speak, Jacques Five!'

The mender of roads, blue cap in hand, wiped his swarthy forehead with it, and said, 'Where shall I commence, monsieur?'

'Commence,' was Monsieur Defarge's not unreasonable reply, 'at the commencement.'

'I saw him then, messieurs,' began the mender of roads, 'a year ago this running summer, underneath the carriage of the Marquis, hanging by the chain. Behold the manner of it. I leaving my work on the road, the sun going to bed, the carriage of the Marquis slowly ascending the hill, he hanging by the chain—like this.'

Again the mender of roads went through the whole performance.

Jacques One struck in, and asked if he had ever seen the man before?

'Never,' answered the mender of roads, recovering his perpendicular.

Jacques Three demanded how he afterwards recognized him then?

'By his tall figure,' said the mender of roads. 'When Monsieur the Marquis demands that evening, "Say, what is he like?" I made response, "Tall as a spectre." '

'You should have said, short as a dwarf,' returned Jacques Two.

'But what did I know? The deed was not then accomplished. I do not offer my testimony. Monsieur the Marquis indicates me with his finger, standing near our little fountain, and says, "To me! Bring that rascal!" My faith, messieurs, I offer nothing.'

'He is right there, Jacques,' murmured Defarge, to him who had interrupted. 'Go on!'

'Good!' said the mender of roads. 'The tall man is lost, and he is sought—how many months? Nine, ten, eleven?'

'No matter, the number,' said Defarge. 'He is well hidden, but at last he is unluckily found. Go on!'

'I am again at work upon the hill-side, and the sun is again about to go to bed. I am collecting my tools to descend to my cottage down in the village below, where it is already dark, when I raise my eyes, and see coming over the hill six soldiers. In the midst of them is a tall man with his arms bound—tied to his sides—like this!'

With the aid of his indispensable cap, he represented a man with his elbows bound fast at his hips, with cords that were knotted behind him.

'I stand aside, messieurs, by my heap of stones, to see the soldiers and their prisoner pass. I do not show the soldiers that I recognize the tall man; he does not show the soldiers that he recognizes me; we do it, and we know it, with our eyes. "Come on!" says the chief of that company, pointing to the village, "bring him fast to his tomb!" and they bring him faster. I follow. His arms are swelled because of being bound so tight, his wooden shoes are large and clumsy, and he is lame. Because he is lame, and consequently slow, they drive him with their guns—like this!'

He imitated the action of a man's being impelled forward by the butt-ends of muskets.

'For some days we see him in the iron cage by the prison.'

He went on, with a wealth of gesture, to tell of the building of a great gallows by the fountain in the village.

'On the top of the gallows is fixed the knife, blade upwards, with its point in the air. He is hanged there forty feet high—and is left hanging, poisoning the water.'

They looked at one another, as he used his blue cap to wipe his face, on which the perspiration had started afresh while he recalled the spectacle.

'It is frightful, messieurs. How can the women and the children draw water! Who can gossip of an evening, under that shadow!

'That's all, messieurs. I left at sunset (as I had been warned to do), and I walked on, that night and half next day, until I met (as I was warned I should) this comrade. With him, I came on.'

After a gloomy silence, the first Jacques said, 'Good! You have acted and recounted faithfully. Will you wait for us a little, outside the door?'

'Very willingly,' said the mender of roads. Whom Defarge escorted to the top of the stairs, and, leaving seated there, returned.

The three had risen, and their heads were together when he came back to the garret.

'How say you, Jacques?' demanded Number One. 'To be registered?'

'To be registered, as doomed to destruction,' returned Defarge.

'The château and all the race?'

'The château and all the race,' returned Defarge. 'Extermination.'

'Are you sure,' asked Jacques Two, of Defarge, 'that no embarrassment can arise from our manner of keeping the register? Without doubt it is safe, for no one beyond ourselves can decipher it; but shall we always be able to decipher it—or, I ought to say, will she?'

'Jacques,' returned Defarge, drawing himself up, 'if madame my wife undertook to keep the register in her memory alone, she would not lose a word of it—not a syllable of it. Knitted, in her own stitches and her own symbols, it will always be as plain to her as the sun. Confide in Madame Defarge. It would be easier for the weakest poltroon that lives, to erase himself from existence, than to erase one letter of his name, or crimes from the knitted register of Madame Defarge.'

The following day Defarge set the mender of roads on his long journey back to the village. At the barrier guard-house he spoke with one of the police, with whom he was intimate. Back at the wine-shop, he said to Madame Defarge:

'Jacques of the police tells me that there is another spy commissioned for our quarter. There may be many more, for all that he can say, but he knows of one.'

'Eh well!' said Madame Defarge, raising her eyebrows with a cool business air. 'It is necessary to register him. How do they call that man?'

'He is English.'

'So much the better. His name?'

'Barsad,' said Defarge, making it French by pronunciation. But, he had been so careful to get it accurately, that he then spelt it with perfect correctness.

'Barsad,' repeated madame. 'Good. Christian name?'

'John.'

'John Barsad,' repeated madame, after murmuring it once to herself. 'Good. His appearance; is it known?'

'Age, about forty years; height, about five feet nine; black hair; complexion dark; generally, rather handsome visage; eyes dark, face thin, long, and sallow; nose aquiline, but not straight, having a peculiar inclination towards the left cheek; expression, therefore, sinister.'

'Eh my faith. It is a portrait!' said madame, laughing. 'He shall be registered.'

Next noontide saw the admirable woman in her usual place in the wine-shop, knitting away assiduously. A rose lay beside her, and if she now and then glanced at the flower, it was with no change of her usual preoccupied air. There were a few customers, drinking or not drinking, standing or seated, sprinkled about.

A figure entering at the door threw a shadow on Madame Defarge which she felt to be a new one. She laid down her knitting, and began to pin her rose in her head-dress, before she looked at the figure.

It was curious. The moment Madame Defarge took up the rose, the customers ceased talking, and began gradually to drop out of the wine-shop.

'Good-day, madame,' said the new comer.

'Good-day, monsieur.'

She said it aloud, but added to herself, as she resumed her knitting: 'Hah! Good-day, age about forty, height about five feet nine, black hair, generally rather handsome visage, complexion dark, eyes dark, thin long and sallow face, aquiline nose but not straight, having a peculiar inclination towards the left cheek which imparts a sinister expression! Good-day, one and all!'

'Have the goodness to give me a little glass of old cognac, and a mouthful of cool fresh water, madame.'

Madame complied with a polite air.

'Marvellous cognac this, madame!'

It was the first time it had ever been so complimented, and Madame Defarge knew better. She said, however, that the cognac was flattered, and took up her knitting. The visitor watched her fingers for a few moments, and took the opportunity of observing the place in general.

'You knit with great skill, madame.'

'I am accustomed to it.'

'A pretty pattern too!'

'*You* think so?' said madame, looking at him with a smile.

'Decidedly. May one ask what it is for?'

'Pastime,' said madame, still looking at him with a smile, while her fingers moved nimbly.

'Not for use?'

'That depends. I may find a use for it one day. If I do—well,' said madame, 'I'll use it!'

It was remarkable: but the taste of Saint Antoine seemed to be decidedly opposed to a rose on the headdress of Madame Defarge. Two men had entered separately, and had been about to order drink, when, catching sight of that novelty, they faltered, made a pretence of looking about as if for some friend who was not there, and went away. Nor, of those who had been there when this visitor entered, was there one left. They had all dropped off. The spy had kept his eyes open, but had been able to detect no sign. They had lounged away in a poverty-stricken, purposeless, accidental manner, quite natural and unimpeachable.

'JOHN,' thought madame, checking off her work as her fingers knitted, and her eyes looked at the stranger. 'Stay long enough, and I shall knit "BARSAD" before you go.'

'You have a husband, madame?'

'I have.'

'Children?'

'No children.'

'Business seems bad?'

'Business is very bad; the people are so poor.'

'Ah, the unfortunate, miserable people! So oppressed, too—as you say.'

'As *you* say,' madame retorted, correcting him, and deftly knitting an extra something into his name that boded him no good.

'Pardon me; certainly it was I who said so, but you naturally think so. Of course.'

'*I* think?' returned madame, in a high voice. 'I and my husband have enough to do to keep this wine-shop open, without thinking.'

The spy, who was there to pick up any crumbs he could find or make, did not allow his baffled state to express itself in his sinister face; but, stood with an air of gossiping gallantry, leaning his elbow on Madame Defarge's little counter, and occasionally sipping his cognac.

'A bad business this, madame, of Gaspard's execution. Ah! the poor Gaspard!' With a sigh of great compassion.

'My faith!' returned madame, coolly and lightly, 'if people use knives for such purposes, they have to pay for it. He knew beforehand what the price of his luxury was; he has paid the price.'

'I believe,' said the spy, dropping his soft voice to a tone that invited confidence, 'I believe there is much compassion and anger in this neighbourhood, touching the poor fellow? Between ourselves.'

'Is there?' asked madame, vacantly.

'Is there not?'

'—Here is my husband!' said Madame Defarge.

As the keeper of the wine-shop entered at the door, the

spy saluted him by touching his hat, and saying, with an engaging smile, 'Good-day, Jacques!' Defarge stopped short, and stared at him.

'Good-day, Jacques!' the spy repeated; with not quite so much confidence, or quite so easy a smile under the stare.

'You deceive yourself, monsieur,' returned the keeper of the wine-shop. 'You mistake me for another. That is not my name. I am Ernest Defarge.'

'It is all the same,' said the spy, airily, but discomfited too: 'good-day!'

'Good-day!' answered Defarge, drily.

Having said it, he passed behind the little counter, and stood with his hand on the back of his wife's chair. The spy, well used to his business, did not change his unconscious attitude, but drained his little glass of cognac, took a sip of fresh water, and asked for another glass of cognac. Madame Defarge poured it out for him, took to her knitting again, and hummed a little song over it.

'The pleasure of conversing with you, Monsieur Defarge, recalls to me,' pursued the spy, 'that I have the honour of cherishing some interesting associations with your name.'

'Indeed!' said Defarge, with much indifference.

'Yes, indeed. When Dr. Manette was released, you, his old domestic, had the charge of him, I know. He was delivered to you. You see I am informed of the circumstances?'

'Such is the fact, certainly,' said Defarge. He had had it conveyed to him, in an accidental touch of his wife's elbow as she knitted and warbled, that he would do best to answer, but always with brevity.

'It was to you,' said the spy, 'that his daughter came; and it was from your care that his daughter took him over to England.'

'Such is the fact,' repeated Defarge.

'Very interesting remembrances!' said the spy. 'I have known Dr. Manette and his daughter, in England.'

'Yes?' said Defarge.

'You don't hear much about them now?' said the spy.

'No,' said Defarge.

'In effect,' madame struck in, looking up from her work and her little song, 'we never hear about them. We received the news of their safe arrival, and perhaps another letter, or perhaps two; but, since then, they have gradually taken their road in life—we, ours—and we have held no correspondence.'

'Perfectly so, madame,' replied the spy. 'She is going to be married.'

'Going?' echoed madame. 'She was pretty enough to have been married long ago. You English are cold, it seems to me.'

'Oh! You know I am English.'

'I perceive your tongue is,' returned madame; 'and what the tongue is, I suppose the man is.'

He did not take the identification as a compliment; but he made the best of it, and turned it off with a laugh. After sipping his cognac to the end, he added:

'Yes, Miss Manette is going to be married. But not to an Englishman; to one who, like herself, is French by birth. And speaking of Gaspard (ah, poor Gaspard! It was cruel, cruel!), it is a curious thing that she is going to marry the nephew of Monsieur the Marquis, for whom Gaspard was exalted to that height of so many feet; in other words, the present Marquis. But he lives unknown in England, he is no Marquis there; he is Mr. Charles Darnay. D'Aulnais is the name of his mother's family.'

Madame Defarge knitted steadily, but the intelligence had

an effect upon her husband. Do what he would, behind the little counter, as to the striking of a light and the lighting of his pipe, he was troubled, and his hand was not trustworthy. The spy would have been no spy if he had failed to see it, or to record it in his mind.

Having made, at least, this one hit, whatever it might prove to be worth, and no customers coming in to help him to any other, Mr. Barsad paid for what he had drunk, and took his leave. For some minutes after he had emerged into the air of Saint Antoine, the husband and wife remained exactly as he had left them, lest he should come back.

'Can it be true,' said Defarge, in a low voice, looking down at his wife as he stood with his hand on the back of her chair; 'what he has said of Ma'amselle Manette?'

'As he has said it,' returned madame, lifting her eye-brows a little, 'it is probably false. But it may be true.'

'If it is——' Defarge began, and stopped.

'If it is?' repeated his wife.

'—And if it does come—I hope, for her sake, Destiny will keep her husband out of France.'

'Her husband's destiny,' said Madame Defarge, with her usual composure, 'will take him where he is to go, and will lead him to the end that is to end him. That is all I know.'

'But it is very strange—now, at least, is it not very strange' —said Defarge, rather pleading with his wife to induce her to admit it, 'that, after all our sympathy for Monsieur her father, and herself, her husband's name should be proscribed under your hand at this moment, by the side of that infernal dog's who had just left us?'

'Stranger things than that will happen when it does come,' answered madame. 'I have them both here, of a certainty; and they are both here for their merits; that is enough.'

She rolled up her knitting when she had said those words, and presently took the rose out of the handkerchief that was wound about her head.

---

10 · NINE DAYS

THE marriage-day was shining brightly, and they were ready outside the closed door of the Doctor's room, where he was speaking with Charles Darnay. They were ready to go to church; the beautiful bride, Mr. Lorry, and Miss Pross.

'And so,' said Mr. Lorry, who could not sufficiently admire the bride, and who had been moving round her to take in every point of her quiet, pretty dress; 'and so it was for this, my sweet Lucie, that I brought you across the Channel, such a baby! Lord bless me! How little I thought what I was doing! How lightly I valued the obligation I was conferring on my friend Mr. Charles!'

'You didn't mean it,' remarked the matter-of-fact Miss Pross, 'and therefore how could you know it? Nonsense!'

'Really? Well; but don't cry,' said the gentle Mr. Lorry.

'I am not crying,' said Miss Pross; '*you* are.'

'I, my Pross?' (By this time, Mr. Lorry dared to be pleasant with her, on occasion.)

'You were, just now; I saw you do it, and I don't wonder at it. Such a present as you have made 'em, is enough to bring tears to anybody's eyes.'

'Ah, well,' said Mr. Lorry. 'Dear me! This is an occasion that makes a man speculate on all he has lost. Dear, dear,

dear! To think that there might have been a Mrs. Lorry, any time these fifty years almost!'

'Not at all!' From Miss Pross.

'You think there never might have been a Mrs. Lorry?' asked the gentleman of that name.

'Pooh!' rejoined Miss Pross; 'you were a bachelor in your cradle.'

'Well!' observed Mr. Lorry, beaming, 'that seems probable, too.'

'And you were cut out for a bachelor,' pursued Miss Pross, 'before you were put in your cradle.'

'Then, I think,' said Mr. Lorry, 'that I was very unhandsomely dealt with, and that I ought to have had a voice in the selection of my pattern. Enough! Now, my dear Lucie,' drawing his arm soothingly round her waist, 'I hear them moving in the next room, and Miss Pross and I, as two formal folks of business, are anxious to say something to you that you wish to hear. You leave your good father, my dear, in hands as loving as your own; he shall be taken every care of; during the next fortnight, while you are in Warwickshire, even Tellson's shall go to the wall (comparatively speaking) before him. And when, at the fortnight's end, he comes to join you and your beloved husband, on your other fortnight's trip in Wales, you shall say that we have sent him to you in the best health and in the happiest frame. Now I hear Somebody's step coming to the door. Let me kiss my dear girl with an old-fashioned bachelor blessing, before Somebody comes to claim his own.'

The door of the Doctor's room opened, and he came out with Charles Darnay. He was so deadly pale—which had not been the case when they went in together—that no vestige of colour was to be seen in his face. But, in the composure of his manner he was unaltered, except that to the shrewd glance of Mr. Lorry it disclosed that the old air of avoidance and dread had lately passed over him, like a cold wind.

He gave his arm to his daughter, and took her downstairs to the chariot. The rest followed in another carriage, and soon, in a neighbouring church, where no strange eyes looked on, Charles Darnay and Lucie Manette were happily married.

They returned home to breakfast, and all went well, and in due course the golden hair that had mingled with the poor shoemaker's white locks in the Paris garret, were mingled with them again in the morning sunlight, on the threshold of the door at parting.

It was a hard parting, though it was not for long. But her father cheered her, and said at last, gently disengaging himself from her enfolding arms, 'Take her, Charles! She is yours!'

The corner being out of the way of the idle and curious, and the preparations having been very simple and few, the Doctor, Mr. Lorry, and Miss Pross, were left quite alone. It was when they turned into the welcome shade of the cool old hall, that Mr. Lorry observed a great change to have come over the Doctor.

It was the old scared lost look that troubled Mr. Lorry; and through his absent manner of clasping his head and drearily wandering away into his own room when they got up-stairs, Mr. Lorry was reminded of Defarge the wine-shop keeper, and the starlight ride.

'I think,' he whispered to Miss Pross, after anxious consideration, 'I think we had best not speak to him just now, or at all disturb him. I must look in at Tellson's; so I will go there at once and come back presently. Then, we will take him a ride into the country, and dine there, and all will be well.'

It was easier for Mr. Lorry to look in at Tellson's, than to look out of Tellson's. He was detained two hours. When he came back, he ascended the old staircase alone, having asked no question of the servant; going thus into the Doctor's rooms, he was stopped by a low sound of knocking.

'Good God!' he said, with a start. 'What's that?'

Miss Pross, with a terrified face, was at his ear. 'O me, O me! All is lost!' cried she, wringing her hands. 'What is to be told to Ladybird? He doesn't know me, and is making shoes!'

Mr. Lorry said what he could to calm her, and went himself into the Doctor's room. The bench was turned towards the light, as it had been when he had seen the shoemaker at his work before, and his head was bent down, and he was very busy.

For nine days the Doctor was again the shoemaker. Mr. Lorry and Miss Pross watched over him and tended him lovingly. Lucie was told in a letter from Miss Pross that he had been called away professionally.

On the tenth day he recovered. They passed the day in the country, and the Doctor was quite restored. On the three following days he remained perfectly well, and on the fourteenth day he went away to join Lucie and her husband. The precaution that had been taken to account for his silence, Mr. Lorry had previously explained to him, and he had written to Lucie in accordance with it, and she had no suspicions.

When the newly-married pair came home, the first person who appeared, to offer his congratulations, was Sydney

Carton. They had not been at home many hours, when he presented himself. He was not improved in habits, or in looks, or in manner; but there was a certain rugged air of fidelity about him.

He watched his opportunity of taking Darnay aside into a window, and of speaking to him when no one overheard.

'Mr. Darnay,' said Carton, 'I wish we might be friends.'

'We are already friends, I hope.'

'You are good enough to say so, as a fashion of speech; but, I don't mean any fashion of speech. At any rate you know me as a dissolute dog who has never done any good, and never will.'

'I don't know that you "never will." '

'But I do, and you must take my word for it. Well! If you could endure to have such a worthless fellow, and a fellow of such indifferent reputation, coming and going at odd times, I should ask that I might be permitted to come and go as a privileged person here; that I might be regarded as an useless (and I would add, if it were not for the resemblance I detected between you and me), an unornamental, piece of furniture, tolerated for its old service, and taken no notice of. I doubt if I should abuse the permission. It is a hundred to one if I should avail myself of it four times a year. It would satisfy me, I dare say, to know that I had it.'

'Will you try?'

'That is another way of saying that I am placed on the footing I have indicated. I thank you, Darnay. I may use that freedom with your name?'

'I think so, Carton, by this time.'

They shook hands upon it, and Sydney turned away. Within a minute afterwards, he was, to all outward appearance, as unsubstantial as ever.

When he was gone, Charles Darnay made some mention of this conversation in general terms, and spoke of Sydney Carton as a problem of carelessness and recklessness. He spoke of him, in short, not bitterly or meaning to bear hard upon him, but as anybody might who saw him as he showed himself.

He had no idea that this could dwell in the thoughts of his fair young wife; but, when he afterwards joined her in their own rooms, he found her waiting for him with the old pretty lifting of the forehead strongly marked.

'We are thoughtful to-night!' said Darnay, drawing his arm about her.

'Yes, dearest Charles,' with the inquiring and attentive expression fixed upon him; 'we are rather thoughtful to-night, for we have something on our mind to-night.'

'What is it, my Lucie?'

'Will you promise not to press one question on me, if I beg you not to ask it?'

'Will I promise? What will I not promise to my Love?'

'I think, Charles, poor Mr. Carton deserves more consideration and respect than you expressed for him to-night.'

'Indeed, my own? Why so?'

'That is what you are not to ask me. But I think—I know—he does.'

'If you know it, it is enough. What would you have me do, my Life?'

'I would ask you, dearest, to be very generous with him always, and very lenient on his faults when he is not by. I would ask you to believe that he has a heart he very, very seldom reveals, and that there are deep wounds in it.'

'It is a painful reflection to me,' said Charles Darnay, quite astounded, 'that I should have done him any wrong. I never thought this of him.'

'My husband, it is so. I fear he is not to be reclaimed; there is scarcely a hope that anything in his character or fortunes is reparable now. But, I am sure that he is capable of good things, gentle things, even magnanimous things.'

She looked so beautiful in the purity of her faith in this lost man, that her husband could have looked at her as she was for hours.

'And, O my dearest Love!' she urged, clinging nearer to him, 'remember how strong we are in our happiness, and how weak he is in his misery!'

The supplication touched him home. 'I will always remember it, dear Heart! I will remember it as long as I live.'

---

11 · ECHOING FOOTSTEPS

A WONDERFUL corner for echoes, it has been remarked, that corner where the Doctor lived. Ever busily winding the golden thread which bound her husband, and her father, and herself, and her old companion, in a life of quiet bliss, Lucie sat in the still house in the tranquilly resounding corner, listening to the echoing footsteps of years.

At first, there were times, though she was a perfectly happy young wife, when her work would slowly fall from her hands, and her eyes would be dimmed. For, there was something coming in the echoes, something light, afar off, and scarcely audible yet, that stirred her heart too much.

The echoes rarely answered to the actual tread of Sydney Carton. Some half-dozen times a year, at most, he claimed his privilege of coming in uninvited, and would sit among them through the evening, as he had once done often.

To these echoes Lucie, sometimes pensive, sometimes amused and laughing, listened in the echoing corner, until her little daughter was six years old. How near to her heart the echoes of her child's tread came, and those of her own dear father's, always active and self-possessed, and those of her dear husband's, need not be told.

But, there were other echoes, from a distance, that rumbled menacingly in the corner all through this space of time. And it was now, about little Lucie's sixth birthday, that they began to have an awful sound, as of a great storm in France with a dreadful sea rising.

On a night in mid-July, one thousand seven hundred and eighty-nine, Mr. Lorry came in late, from Tellson's, and sat himself down by Lucie and her husband in the dark window. It was a hot, wild night, and they were all three reminded of the old Sunday night when they had looked at the lightning from the same place.

'I began to think,' said Mr. Lorry, 'that I should have to pass the night at Tellson's. We have been so full of business all day, that we have not known what to do first, or which way to turn. There is such an uneasiness in Paris that our customers over there, seem not to be able to confide their property to us fast enough.'

'That has a bad look,' said Darnay.

'A bad look, you say, my dear Darnay? Yes, but we don't know what reason there is in it.'

'Still,' said Darnay, 'you know how gloomy and threatening the sky is.'

'I know that, to be sure,' assented Mr. Lorry, trying to persuade himself that his sweet temper was soured, and that he grumbled, 'but I am determined to be peevish after my long day's botheration. Where is Manette?'

'Here he is,' said the Doctor, entering the dark room at the moment.

'I am quite glad you are at home; for these hurries and forebodings by which I have been surrounded all day long, have made me nervous without reason. You are not going out, I hope?'

'No; I am going to play backgammon with you, if you like,' said the Doctor.

'I don't think I do like, if I may speak my mind. I am not fit to be pitted against you to-night. Is the teaboard still there, Lucie? Thank ye. Now, come and take your place in the circle, and let us sit quiet, and hear the echoes about which you have your theory.'

'Not a theory; it was a fancy.'

'A fancy, then, my wise pet,' said Mr. Lorry, patting her hand. 'They are very numerous and very loud, though, are they not? Only hear them!'

Headlong, mad, and dangerous footsteps to force their way into anybody's life, footsteps not easily made clean again if once stained red, the footsteps raging in Saint Antoine afar off, as the little circle sat in the dark London window.

Saint Antoine had been, that morning, a vast dusky mass of scarecrows heaving to and fro, with frequent gleams of light above the billowy heads, where steel blades and bayonets shone in the sun. A tremendous roar arose from the throat of Saint Antoine, and a forest of naked arms struggled in the air like shrivelled branches of trees in a winter wind: all the fingers convulsively clutching at every weapon or semblance of a weapon that was thrown up from the depths below.

Who gave them out, whence they came, no eye in the throng could have told; but muskets were being distributed —so were cartridges, powder, and ball, bars of iron and wood, knives, axes, pikes, every possible weapon. People who could lay hold of nothing else, set themselves with bleeding hands to force stones and bricks out of their places in walls.

As a whirlpool of boiling waters has a centre point, so, all this raging circled round Defarge's wine-shop, and every human drop in the caldron had a tendency to be sucked towards the vortex where Defarge himself, already begrimed with gunpowder and sweat, issued orders, issued arms, laboured and strove in the thickest of the uproar.

'Keep near to me, Jacques Three,' cried Defarge; 'and do you, Jacques One and Two, separate and put yourselves at the head of as many of these patriots as you can. Where is my wife?'

'Eh, well! Here you see me!' said madame, composed as ever, but not knitting to-day. Madame's resolute right hand was occupied with an axe, in place of the usual softer implements, and in her girdle were a pistol and a cruel knife.

'Where do you go, my wife?'

'I go,' said madame, 'with you at present. You shall see me at the head of women, by-and-by.'

'Come, then!' cried Defarge, in a resounding voice. 'Patriots and friends, we are ready! The Bastille!'

With a roar the living sea rose, wave on wave, depth on depth, and overflowed the city to that point. Alarm-bells ringing, drums beating, the sea raging and thundering on its new beach, the attack began.

Deep ditches, double drawbridge, massive stone walls,

eight great towers, cannon, muskets, fire and smoke. Through the fire and through the smoke—in the fire and in the smoke, for the sea cast him up against a cannon, and on the instant he became a cannonier—Defarge of the wine-shop worked like a manful soldier. Two fierce hours.

Deep ditch, single drawbridge, massive stone walls, eight great towers, cannon, muskets, fire and smoke. One drawbridge down! 'Work, comrades all, work! Work, Jacques One, Jacques Two, Jacques One Thousand, Jacques Two Thousand, Jacques Five-and-Twenty Thousand; in the name of all the Angels or the Devils—which you prefer—work!' Thus Defarge of the wine-shop, still at his gun, which had long grown hot.

'To me, women!' cried madame his wife. 'What! We can kill as well as the men when the place is taken!'

Cannon, muskets, fire and smoke; but, still the deep ditch, the single drawbridge, the massive stone walls, and the eight great towers. Slight displacements of the raging sea, made by the falling wounded. Flashing weapons, shrieks, volleys, execrations, bravery without stint, and the furious sounding of the living sea; and still Defarge of the wine-shop at his gun, grown doubly hot by the service of four fierce hours.

A white flag from within the fortress, and a parley—suddenly the sea rose immeasurably wider and higher and swept Defarge of the wine-shop over the lowered drawbridge, past the massive stone outer walls, in among the eight great towers surrendered!

So resistless was the force of the ocean bearing him on, that even to draw his breath or turn his head was impracticable, until he was landed in the outer court-yard of the Bastille. There, against an angle of a wall, he made a struggle to look about him. Jacques Three was nearly at his side; Madame Defarge, still heading some of her women, was visible in the inner distance, and her knife was in her hand. Everywhere was tumult, exultation, astounding noise.

'The Prisoners!'

'The Records!'

'The secret cells!'

'The instruments of torture!'

Of all these cries, 'The Prisoners!' was the cry most taken up by the sea that rushed in. When the foremost billows rolled past, Defarge laid his strong hand on one of the prison officers—a man with a grey head, who had a lighted torch in his hand—separated him from the rest and got him between himself and the wall.

'What is the meaning of One Hundred and Five, North Tower?' asked Defarge. 'Quick!'

'Monsieur, it is a cell.'

'Show it me!'

Through gloomy vaults where the light of day had never shone, past hideous doors, down cavernous flights of steps, and again up steep rugged ascents of stone, Defarge, the turnkey, and Jacques Three went with all the speed they could make.

The turnkey stopped at a low door, put a key in a clashing lock, swung the door slowly open, and said, as they all bent their heads and passed in:

'One hundred and five, North Tower!'

There was a small, heavily-grated, unglazed window high in the wall, with a stone screen before it, so that the sky could be only seen by stooping low and looking up. There was a small chimney. There was a stool, and table, and a straw bed. There were the four blackened walls, and a rusted iron ring in one of them.

'Pass that torch slowly along these walls, that I may see them,' said Defarge to the turnkey.

The man obeyed, and Defarge followed the light closely with his eyes.

'Stop!—Look here, Jacques!'

'A.M.!' croaked Jacques Three.

'Alexandre Manette,' said Defarge. 'What is that in your hand? A crowbar? Give it me!'

He had still the linstock of his gun in his own hand. He made a sudden exchange of the two instruments, and turning on the worm-eaten stool and table, beat them to pieces in a few blows.

'Hold the light higher!' he said, wrathfully, to the turnkey. 'Look among those fragments with care, Jacques. And see! Here is my knife,' throwing it to him; 'rip open that bed, and search the straw. Hold the light higher, you!'

With a menacing look at the turnkey he crawled upon the hearth, and, peering up the chimney, struck and prised at its sides with the crowbar, and worked at the iron grating across it. In a few minutes, some mortar and dust came dropping down, and in it, and in a crevice in the chimney into which his weapon had slipped or wrought itself, he groped with a cautious touch.

'Nothing in the wood, and nothing in the straw, Jacques?'

'Nothing.'

'Let us collect them together, in the middle of the cell. So! Light them, you!'

The turnkey fired the little pile, which blazed high and hot. Stooping again to come out at the low-arched door, they left it burning, and retraced their way to the courtyard; and into the raging flood once more.

They found it surging and tossing, in quest of Defarge

himself. Saint Antoine was clamorous to have its wine-shop keeper foremost in the guard upon the governor who had defended the Bastille and shot the people. Otherwise, the governor would not be marched to the Hôtel de Ville for judgement.

Prisoners released, gory heads on pikes, the keys of the accursed fortress of the eight strong towers, some discovered letters and other memorials of prisoners of old time, long dead of broken hearts,—such, and such-like, the loudly echoing footsteps of Saint Antoine escort through the Paris streets in mid-July, one thousand seven hundred and eighty-nine. Now, Heaven defeat the fancy of Lucie Darnay, and keep these feet far out of her life! For, they are headlong, mad, and dangerous; and in the years so long after the breaking of the cask at Defarge's wine-shop door, they are not easily purified when once stained red.

Haggard Saint Antoine had had only one exultant week, when Madame Defarge, with her arms folded, sat in the morning light and heat, contemplating the wine-shop and the street. In both, there were several knots of loungers, squalid and miserable, but now with a manifest sense of power. The raggedest nightcap, awry on the wretchedest head, had this crooked significance in it: 'I know how hard it has grown for me, the wearer of this, to support life in myself; but do you know how easy it has grown for me, the wearer of this, to destroy life in you?' Every lean bare arm, that had been without work before, had this work always ready for it now, that it could strike. The fingers of the knitting women were vicious, with the experience that they could tear. There was a change in the appearance of Saint Antoine; the image had been hammering into this for hundreds of years, and the last finishing blows had told mightily on the expression.

Monsieur Defarge said to madame his wife, in husky tones:

'At last it is come, my dear!'

'Eh well!' returned madame. 'Almost.'

There was a change on the village where the fountain fell, and where the mender of roads went forth daily to hammer out of the stones on the highway such morsels of bread as might hold his poor body together.

Far and wide lay a ruined country, yielding nothing but desolation. Every green leaf, every blade of grass and blade of grain, was as shrivelled and poor as the miserable people. Everything was bowed down, dejected, oppressed, and broken. Habitations, fences, domestic animals, men, women, children, and the soil that bare them—all worn out.

For scores of years gone by, Monseigneur had squeezed it and wrung it, and had seldom graced it with his presence except for the pleasures of the chase.

The change consisted in the appearance of strange faces, for in these times, as the mender of roads worked, solitary, in the dust, thinking how little he had for supper and how much more he would eat if he had it—in these times, as he raised his eyes from his lonely labour, and viewed the prospect, he would see some rough figure approaching on foot, the like of which was once a rarity in those parts, but was now a frequent presence. As it advanced, the mender of roads would discern without surprise, that it was a shaggy-haired man, of almost barbarian aspect, tall, in wooden shoes that were clumsy even to the eyes of a mender of roads, grim, rough, steeped in the mud and dust of many highways.

Such a man came upon him, like a ghost, at noon in the July weather, as he sat on his heap of stones under a bank, taking such shelter as he could get from a shower of hail.

The man looked at him, looked at the village in the hollow, at the mill, and at the prison on the crag. When he had identified these objects, he said:

'How goes it, Jacques?'

'All well, Jacques.'

'Touch then!'

They joined hands, and the man sat down on the heap of stones.

'No dinner?'

'Nothing but supper now,' said the mender of roads, with a hungry face.

'It is the fashion,' growled the man.

He took out a blackened pipe, filled it, lighted it with flint and steel, pulled at it until it was in a bright glow: then, suddenly held it from him and dropped something into it from between his finger and thumb, that blazed and went out in a puff of smoke.

'Touch then.' It was the turn of the mender of roads to say it this time, after observing these operations. They again joined hands.

'To-night?' said the mender of roads.

'To-night,' said the man, putting the pipe in his mouth.

'Where?'

'Here.'

He and the mender of roads sat on the heap of stones looking silently at one another, with the hail driving in between them, until the sky began to clear over the village.

'Show me!' said the traveller then, moving to the brow of the hill.

'See! About two leagues beyond the summit of that hill beyond the village.'

The wayfarer left him. At sunset the mender of roads went home, and was soon at the fountain, squeezing himself in among the lean kine brought there to drink, and appearing even to whisper to them in his whispering to all the village. When the village had taken its poor supper, it did not creep to bed, as it usually did, but came out of doors again, and remained there. A curious contagion of whispering was upon it, and also, when it gathered together at the fountain in the dark, another curious contagion of looking expectantly at the sky in one direction only.

The night deepened. The trees environing the old château, keeping its solitary state apart, moved in a rising wind, as though they threatened the pile of building, massive and dark in the gloom. Through the woods, four heavy-treading, unkempt figures crushed the high grass and cracked the branches, striding on cautiously to come together in the court-yard. Four lights broke out there, and moved away in different directions, and all was black again.

But, not for long. Presently, the château began to make itself strangely visible by some light of its own, as though it were growing luminous. Then, a flickering streak played behind the architecture of the front, picking out transparent places, and showing where balustrades, arches, and windows were. Then it soared higher, and grew broader and brighter. Soon, from a score of the great windows, fire burst forth.

The château was in flames.

12 · DRAWN TO THE LOADSTONE ROCK

In such risings of fire and risings of sea, three years of tempest were consumed. Three more birthdays of little Lucie had been woven into the peaceful tissue of the life of her home.

Many a night and many a day had its inmates listened to the echoes in the corner, with hearts that failed them when they heard the thronging feet. For, the footsteps had become to their minds as the footsteps of a people changed into wild beasts, by terrible enchantment long persisted in.

The August of the year one thousand seven hundred and ninety-two was come, and Monseigneur was by this time scattered far and wide.

As was natural, the head-quarters and great gathering-place of Monseigneur, in London, was Tellson's Bank.

On a steaming, misty afternoon, Mr. Lorry sat at his desk, and Charles Darnay stood leaning on it, talking with him in a low voice.

'But, although you are the youngest man that ever lived,' said Charles Darnay, rather hesitating, 'I must still suggest to you——'

'I understand. That I am too old?' said Mr. Lorry.

'Unsettled weather, a long journey, uncertain means of travelling, a disorganized country, a city that may not be even safe for you.'

'My dear Charles,' said Mr. Lorry, with cheerful confidence, 'you touch some of the reasons for my going: not for my staying away. It is safe enough for me; nobody will care to interfere with an old fellow of hard upon four-score when there are so many people there much better worth interfering with. As to its being a disorganized city, if it were not a disorganized city there would be no occasion to send somebody from our House here to our House there, who knows the city and the business, of old, and is in Tellson's confidence. As to the uncertain travelling, the long journey, and the winter weather, if I were not prepared to submit myself to a few inconveniences for the sake of Tellson's, after all these years, who ought to be?'

'I wish I were going myself,' said Charles Darnay, somewhat restlessly, and like one thinking aloud.

'Indeed! You are a pretty fellow to object and advise!' exclaimed Mr. Lorry. 'You wish you were going yourself? And you a Frenchman born? You are a wise counsellor.'

'My dear Mr. Lorry, it is because I am a Frenchman born, that the thought (which I did not mean to utter here, however) has passed through my mind often. One cannot help thinking, having had some sympathy for the miserable people, and having abandoned something to them,' he spoke here in his former thoughtful manner, 'that one might be listened to, and might have the power to persuade to some restraint. Only last night, after you had left us, when I was talking to Lucie——'

'When you were talking to Lucie,' Mr. Lorry repeated. 'Yes. I wonder you are not ashamed to mention the name of Lucie! Wishing you were going to France at this time of day!'

'However, I am not going,' said Charles Darnay, with a smile. 'It is more to the purpose that you say you are.'

'And I am, in plain reality. The truth is, my dear Charles, you can have no conception of the difficulty with which our business is transacted, and of the peril in which our books and papers over yonder are involved. The Lord above knows what the compromising consequences would be to numbers of people, if some of our documents were seized or destroyed. Now, a judicious selection from these with the least possible delay, and the burying of them, or otherwise getting of them out of harm's way, is within the power of scarcely anyone but myself, if any one. You are to remember, that getting things out of Paris at this present time, no matter what things, is next to an impossibility. Papers and precious matters were this very day brought to us here by the strangest bearers you can imagine, every one of whom had his head hanging on by a single hair as he passed the Barriers. At another time, our parcels would come and go, as easily as in business-like Old England; but now, everything is stopped.'

'And do you really go to-night?'

'I really go to-night, for the case has become too pressing to admit of delay.'

'And do you take no one with you?'

'All sorts of people have been proposed to me, but I intend to take Jerry. Jerry has been my body-guard on Sunday nights for a long time past, and I am used to him. Nobody will suspect Jerry of being anything but an English bull-dog, or of having any design in his head but to fly at anybody who touches his master.'

The Manager of Tellson's approached Mr. Lorry, and laying a soiled and unopened letter before him, asked if he had yet discovered any traces of the person to whom it was addressed. The Manager laid the letter down so close to Darnay that he saw the direction—the more quickly because it was his own right name. The address, turned into English, ran:

'Very pressing. To Monsieur heretofore the Marquis St.

Evrémonde, of France. Confided to the cares of Messrs. Tellson and Co., Bankers, London, England.'

On the marriage morning, Dr. Manette had made it his one urgent and express request to Charles Darnay, that the secret of this name should be—unless he, the Doctor, dissolved the obligation—kept inviolate between them. Nobody else knew it to be his name; his own wife had no suspicion of the fact; Mr. Lorry could have none.

'No,' said Mr. Lorry, in reply to the Manager; 'I have referred it, I think, to everybody now here, and no one can tell me where this gentleman is to be found.'

The hands of the clock verging upon the hour of closing the Bank, there was a general set of the current of talkers past Mr. Lorry's desk. He held the letter out inquiringly: and Monseigneur looked at it, in the person of this plotting and indignant refugee; and Monseigneur looked at it, in the person of that plotting and indignant refugee; and This, That, and The Other, all had something disparaging to say, in French or in English, concerning the Marquis who was not to be found.

'Nephew, I believe—but in any case degenerate successor—of the polished Marquis who was murdered,' said one. 'Happy to say, I never knew him.'

'A craven who abandoned his post,' said another—this Monseigneur had been got out of Paris, legs uppermost and half suffocated, in a load of hay—'some years ago.'

'Infected with the new doctrines,' said a third, eyeing the direction through his glass in passing; 'set himself in opposition to the last Marquis, abandoned the estates when he inherited them, and left them to the ruffian herd.'

Mr. Lorry and Charles Darnay were left alone at the desk, in the general departure from the Bank.

'I know the fellow,' said Darnay.

'Will you take charge of the letter, then?' said Mr. Lorry. 'You know where to deliver it?'

'I do.'

'Will you undertake to explain, that we suppose it to have been addressed here, on the chance of our knowing where to forward it, and that it has been here some time?'

'I will do so. Do you start for Paris from here?'

'From here, at eight.'

'I will come back, to see you off.'

Very ill at ease with himself, Darnay made the best of his way into the quiet of the Temple, opened the letter, and read it. These were its contents:

'Prison of the Abbaye, Paris.
'June 21, 1792.

'MONSIEUR HERETOFORE THE MARQUIS,

'I have been seized, with great violence and indignity, and brought a long journey on foot to Paris.

'The crime for which I am imprisoned, Monsieur heretofore the Marquis, and for which I shall be summoned before the tribunal, and shall lose my life (without your so generous help), is, they tell me, treason against the majesty of the people, in that I have acted against them for an emigrant. It is in vain I represent that I have acted for them, and not against, according to your commands. It is in vain I represent that I had remitted the imposts they had ceased to pay; that I had collected no rent; that I had had recourse to no process. The only response is, that I have acted for an emigrant, and where is that emigrant?

'Ah! most gracious Monsieur heretofore the Marquis,

where is that emigrant? I cry in my sleep where is he? I ask Heaven, will he not come to deliver me?

'For the love of Heaven, I pray you, Monsieur heretofore the Marquis, to help me. My fault is, that I have been true to you.

'From this prison here of horror, whence I every hour tend nearer and nearer to destruction,

'Your afflicted

GABELLE.'

The latent uneasiness in Darnay's mind was roused to vigorous life by this letter. The peril of an old servant and a good one, whose only crime was fidelity to himself and his family, stared him reproachfully in the face. He knew very well, that in his love for Lucie, his renunciation of his social place had been hurried and incomplete. He knew that he ought to have systematically worked it out and supervised it, and that he had meant to do it, and that it had never been done.

But, he had oppressed no man, he had imprisoned no man; he was so far from having harshly exacted payment of his dues, that he had relinquished them of his own will, thrown himself on a world with no favour in it, won his own private place there, and earned his own bread. Monsieur Gabelle had held the impoverished and involved estate on written instructions, to spare the people, to give them what little there was to give. This favoured the desperate resolution Charles Darnay had begun to make, that he would go to Paris.

Yes. Like the mariner in the old story, the winds and streams had driven him within the influence of the Loadstone Rock, and it was drawing him to itself, and he must go.

As he walked to and fro with his resolution made, he considered that neither Lucie nor her father must know of it until he was gone. Lucie should be spared the pain of separation; and her father, always reluctant to turn his thoughts towards the dangerous ground of old, should come to the knowledge of the step, as a step taken, and not in the balance of suspense and doubt.

He walked to and fro, with thoughts very busy, until it was time to return to Tellson's and take leave of Mr. Lorry. As soon as he arrived in Paris he would present himself to this old friend, but he must say nothing of his intention now.

A carriage with post-horses was ready at the Bank door, and Jerry was booted and equipped.

'I have delivered that letter,' said Charles Darnay to Mr. Lorry. 'I would not consent to your being charged with any written answer, but perhaps you will take a verbal one?'

'That I will, and readily,' said Mr. Lorry, 'if it is not dangerous.'

'Not at all. Though it is to a prisoner in the Abbaye.'

'What is his name?' said Mr. Lorry, with his open pocket-book in his hand.

'Gabelle.'

'Gabelle. And what is the message to the unfortunate Gabelle in prison?'

'Simply, "that he has received the letter, and will come." '

'Any time mentioned?'

'He will start upon his journey to-morrow night.'

'Any person mentioned?'

'No.'

He helped Mr. Lorry to wrap himself in a number of coats and cloaks, and went out with him from the warm atmosphere of the old Bank, into the misty air. 'My love to

Lucie, and to little Lucie,' said Mr. Lorry at parting, 'and take precious care of them till I come back.' Charles Darnay shook his head and doubtfully smiled, as the carriage rolled away.

That night—it was the fourteenth of August—he sat up late, and wrote two fervent letters; one was to Lucie, explaining the strong obligation he was under to go to Paris, and showing her the reasons that he had, for feeling confident that he could become involved in no personal danger there; the other was to the Doctor, confiding Lucie and their dear child to his care, and dwelling on the same topics with the strongest assurances. To both, he wrote that he would despatch letters in proof of his safety, immediately after his arrival.

It was a hard day, that day of being among them, with the first reservation of their joint lives on his mind. It was a hard matter to preserve the innocent deceit of which they were profoundly unsuspicious. But, an affectionate glance at his wife, so happy and busy, made him resolute not to tell her what impended, and the day passed quickly away. Early in the evening he embraced her, and her scarcely less dear namesake, pretending that he would return by-and-by (an imaginary engagement took him out, and he had secreted a valise of clothes ready), and so he emerged into the heavy mist of the heavy streets, with a heavier heart.

The unseen force was drawing him fast to itself, now, and all the tides and winds were setting straight and strong towards it. He left his two letters with a trusty porter, to be delivered half an hour before midnight, and no sooner; took horse for Dover; and began his journey.

13 · IN SECRET

THE traveller fared slowly on his way, who fared towards Paris from England in the autumn of the year one thousand seven hundred and ninety-two. Every town-gate and village taxing-house had its band of citizen-patriots, with their national muskets in a most explosive state of readiness, who stopped all comers and goers, cross-questioned them, inspected their papers, looked for their names in lists of their own, turned them back, or sent them on, or stopped them and laid them in hold, as their capricious judgement or fancy deemed best for the dawning Republic One and Indivisible, of Liberty, Equality, Fraternity, or Death.

Charles Darnay soon perceived that for him along these country roads there was no hope of return until he should have been declared a good citizen at Paris. Whatever might befall now, he must on to his journey's end. Not a mean village closed upon him, not a common barrier dropped across the road behind him, but he knew it to be another iron door in the series that was barred between him and England.

The universal watchfulness not only stopped him on the highway twenty times in a stage, but retarded his progress twenty times in a day, by riding after him and taking him back, riding before him and stopping him, riding with him and keeping him in charge. He had been days upon his journey in France alone, when he went to bed tired out, in a little town on the high road, still a long way from Paris.

Nothing but the production of the afflicted Gabelle's letter from his prison of the Abbaye would have got him on so far. His difficulty at the guard-house in this small place had been such, that he felt his journey to have come to a crisis.

And he was, therefore, as little surprised as a man could be, to find himself awakened in the middle of the night.

Awakened by a timid local functionary and three armed patriots in rough red caps and with pipes in their mouths, who sat down on the bed.

'Emigrant,' said the functionary, 'I am going to send you on to Paris, under an escort.'

'Citizen, I desire nothing more than to get to Paris, though I could dispense with the escort.'

'Silence!' growled a red-cap, striking at the coverlet with the butt-end of his musket. 'Peace, aristocrat!'

'It is as the good patriot says,' observed the timid functionary. 'You are an aristocrat, and must have an escort—and must pay for it.'

'I have no choice,' said Charles Darnay.

'You have no choice,' observed the functionary. 'Rise and dress yourself, emigrant.'

Darnay complied, and was taken back to the guard-house, where other patriots in rough red caps were smoking, drinking, and sleeping, by a watch-fire. Here he paid a heavy price for his escort, and hence he started with it on the wet, wet roads at three o'clock in the morning.

The escort were two mounted patriots in red caps and tricoloured cockades, armed with national muskets and sabres, who rode one on either side of him. In this state they traversed without change, except of horses and pace, all the mire-deep leagues that lay between them and the capital.

They travelled in the night, halting an hour or two after daybreak, and lying by until the twilight fell.

Daylight at last found them before the wall of Paris. The barrier was closed and strongly guarded when they rode up to it.

'Where are the papers of this prisoner?' demanded a resolute-looking man in authority, who was summoned out by the guard.

Naturally struck by the disagreeable word, Charles Darnay requested the speaker to take notice that he was a free traveller and French citizen, in charge of an escort which the disturbed state of the country had imposed upon him, and which he had paid for.

'Where,' repeated the same personage, without taking any heed of him whatever, 'are the papers of this prisoner?'

The drunken patriot had them in his cap, and produced them. Casting his eyes over Gabelle's letter, the same personage in authority showed surprise, and looked at Darnay with a close attention.

He left escort and escorted without saying a word, however, and went into the guard-room; meanwhile, they sat upon their horses outside the gate.

When he had sat in his saddle some half-hour, Darnay found himself confronted by the same man in authority, who requested him to dismount. He accompanied him into a guard-room, smelling of common wine and tobacco, where certain soldiers and patriots, asleep and awake, drunk and sober, were standing and lying about. Some registers were lying open on a desk, and an officer presided over these.

'Citizen Defarge,' said he to Darnay's conductor, as he took a slip of paper to write on. 'Is this the emigrant Evrémonde?'

'This is the man.'

'Your age, Evrémonde?'

'Thirty-seven.'

'You are consigned, Evrémonde, to the prison of La Force.'

'Just Heaven!' exclaimed Darnay. 'Under what law, and for what offence?'

The officer looked up from his slip of paper for a moment.

'We have new laws, Evrémonde, and new offences, since you were here.' He said it with a hard smile, and went on writing.

'I entreat you to observe that I have come here voluntarily, in response to that written appeal to help a fellow-countryman which lies before you. I demand no more than the opportunity to do so without delay. Is not that my right?'

'Emigrants have no rights, Evrémonde,' was the stolid reply. The officer wrote until he had finished, and handed it to Defarge, with the words 'In secret'.

Defarge motioned with the paper to the prisoner that he must accompany him. The prisoner obeyed, and a guard of two armed patriots attended them.

'Is it you,' said Defarge, in a low voice, as they went down the guard-house steps and turned into Paris, 'who married the daughter of Doctor Manette, once a prisoner in the Bastille?'

'Yes,' replied Darnay, looking at him with surprise.

'My name is Defarge, and I keep a wine-shop in the Quarter Saint Antoine. Possibly you have heard of me.'

'My wife came to your house to reclaim her father? Yes!'

'In the name of that sharp female newly-born, and called La Guillotine, why did you come to France?'

'You heard me say why, a minute ago. Do you not believe it is the truth?'

'A bad truth for you,' said Defarge, speaking with knitted brows, and looking straight before him.

'Will you answer me a single question?'

'Perhaps. According to its nature. You can say what it is.'

'In this prison that I am going to so unjustly, shall I have some free communication with the world outside?'

'You will see.'

'I am not to be buried there, prejudged, and without any means of presenting my case?'

'You will see. But, what then? Other people have been similarly buried in worse prisons, before now.'

'But never by me, Citizen Defarge.'

Defarge glanced darkly at him for answer, and walked on in a steady and set silence. In silence they arrived at the prison of La Force.

A man with a bloated face opened the strong wicket, to whom Defarge presented 'The Emigrant Evrémonde. In secret.'

'What the Devil! How many more of them!' exclaimed the man with the bloated face.

Defarge took his receipt without noticing the exclamation, and withdrew, with his two fellow-patriots.

'What the Devil, I say again!' exclaimed the gaoler. 'How many more! Come with me, emigrant.'

Through the dismal prison twilight, his new charge accompanied him by corridor and staircase, many doors clanging and locking behind them until they came to a grated door.

The wicket opened on a stone staircase, leading upward. When they had ascended forty steps (the prisoner already counted them), the gaoler opened a low black door, and they passed into a solitary cell. It struck cold and damp but was not dark.

'Yours,' said the gaoler.

'Why am I confined alone?'

'How do I know!'

'I can buy pen, ink, and paper?'

'Such are not my orders. You will be visited, and can ask then. At present, you may buy your food, and nothing more.'

There were in the cell, a chair, a table, and a straw mattress. The gaoler made a general inspection of these objects, and of the four walls, before going out.

Tellson's Bank, established in the Saint Germain Quarter of Paris, was in a wing of a large house, approached by a court-yard and shut off from the street by a high wall and a strong gate.

Mr. Jarvis Lorry sat by a newly-lighted wood fire (the blighted and unfruitful year was prematurely cold), and on his honest and courageous face there was a deeper shade than the pendent lamp could throw—a shade of horror.

He occupied rooms in the Bank, in his fidelity to the House of which he had grown to be a part, like a strong root-ivy. On the opposite side of the court-yard, under a colonnade, was extensive standing for carriages—where, indeed, some carriages yet stood. Against two of the pillars were fastened two great flaring flambeaux, and in the light of these, standing out in the open air, was a large grindstone: a roughly mounted thing which appeared to have hurriedly been brought there from some neighbouring smithy, or other workshop. Rising and looking out of the window at these harmless objects, Mr. Lorry shivered, and retired to his seat by the fire. He had opened, not only the glass window, but the lattice blind outside it, and he had closed both again, and he shivered through his frame.

From the streets beyond the high wall and the strong gate,

there came the usual night hum of the city, with now and then an indescribable ring in it, weird and unearthly.

'Thank God,' said Mr. Lorry, clasping his hands, 'that no one near and dear to me is in this dreadful town to-night. May He have mercy on all who are in danger!'

Soon afterwards, the bell at the great gate sounded, and he thought, 'They have come back!' and sat listening. But, there was no loud irruption into the court-yard, as he had expected, and he heard the gate clash again, and all was quiet.

The nervousness and dread that were upon him inspired that vague uneasiness respecting the Bank, which a great change would naturally awaken. It was well guarded, and he got up to go among the trusty people who were watching it, when his door suddenly opened, and two figures rushed in, at sight of which he fell back in amazement.

Lucie and her father! Lucie with her arms stretched out to him, and with that old look of earnestness concentrated and intensified.

'What is this?' cried Mr. Lorry, breathless and confused. 'What is the matter? Lucie! Manette! What has happened? What has brought you here? What is it?'

With the look fixed upon him, she panted out imploringly, 'O my dear friend! My husband!'

'Your husband, Lucie?'

'Here.'

'Here, in Paris?'

'Has been here for some days—three or four—I don't know how many—I can't collect my thoughts. An errand of generosity brought him here unknown to us; he was stopped at the barrier, and sent to prison.'

The old man uttered an irrepressible cry. Almost at the

same moment, the bell of the great gate rang again, and a loud noise of feet and voices came pouring into the courtyard.

'What is that noise?' said the Doctor, turning towards the window.

'Don't look!' cried Mr. Lorry. 'Don't look out! Manette, for your life, don't touch the blind!'

The Doctor turned, with his hand upon the fastening of the window, and said, with a cool bold smile:

'My dear friend, I have a charmed life in this city. I have been a Bastille prisoner. There is no patriot in Paris who, knowing me to have been a prisoner in the Bastille, would touch me, except to overwhelm me with embraces, or carry me in triumph. My old pain has given me a power that has brought us through the barrier, and gained us news of Charles there, and brought us here. I knew it would be so; I knew I could help Charles out of all danger; I told Lucie so.—What is that noise?' His hand was again upon the window.

'Don't look!' cried Mr. Lorry, absolutely desperate. 'No, Lucie, my dear, nor you!' He got his arm round her, and held her. 'Don't be so terrified, my love. I solemnly swear to you that I know of no harm having happened to Charles; that I had no suspicion even of his being in this fatal place. What prison is he in?'

'La Force!'

'La Force! Lucie, my child, if ever you were brave and serviceable in your life—and you were always both—you will do exactly as I bid you; for more depends upon it than you can think. There is no help for you in any action on your part to-night; you cannot possibly stir out. You must let me put you in a room at the back here. You must leave your father and me alone for two minutes, and as there are Life and Death in the world you must not delay.'

'I will be submissive to you. I see in your face that you know I can do nothing else than this. I know you are true.'

The old man kissed her, and hurried her into his room, and turned the key; then, came hurrying back to the Doctor, and opened the window and partly opened the blind, and put his hand upon the Doctor's arm, and looked out with him into the court-yard.

Looked out upon a throng of men and women: the people in possession of the house had let them in at the gate, and they rushed in to work at the grindstone; it had evidently been set up there for their purpose, as in a convenient and retired spot.

But, such awful workers, and such awful work!

The grindstone had a double handle, and, turning at it madly were two men, whose faces, as their long hair flapped back when the whirlings of the grindstone brought their faces up, were more horrible and cruel than the visages of the wildest savages in their most barbarous disguise. As these ruffians turned and turned, their matted locks now flung forward over their eyes, now flung backward over their necks, some women held wine to their mouths that they might drink; and what with dropping blood, and what with dropping wine, and what with the stream of sparks struck out of the stone, all their wicked atmosphere seemed gore and fire. The eye could not detect one creature in the group free from the smear of blood. Shouldering one another to get next at the sharpening-stone, were men stripped to the waist, with the stain all over their limbs and bodies; men in all sorts of rags, with the stain upon those rags; men devilishly set off with spoils of women's lace and silk and ribbon, with the stain dyeing those trifles through and through. Hatchets, knives, bayonets, swords, all brought to be sharpened, were all red with it. And as the frantic wielders of these weapons snatched them from the stream of sparks and tore away into the streets, the same red hue was red in their frenzied eyes.

All this was seen in a moment. They drew back from the window, and the Doctor looked for explanation in his friend's ashy face.

'They are,' Mr. Lorry whispered the words, 'murdering the prisoners. If you are sure of what you say; if you really have the power you think you have—as I believe you have—make yourself known to these devils, and get taken to La Force. It may be too late, I don't know, but let it not be a minute later!'

Doctor Manette pressed his hand, hastened bareheaded out of the room, and was in the court-yard when Mr. Lorry regained the blind.

His streaming white hair, his remarkable face, and the impetuous confidence of his manner, as he put the weapons aside like water, carried him in an instant to the heart of the concourse at the stone. For a few moments there was a pause, and a flurry, and a murmur; and then Mr. Lorry saw him, surrounded by all, and in the midst of a line of twenty men long, all linked shoulder to shoulder, and hand to shoulder, hurried out with cries of—'Live the Bastille Prisoner! Help for the Bastille prisoner's kindred in La Force! Room for the Bastille prisoner in front there!'

He closed the lattice again with a fluttering heart, closed the window and the curtain, hastened to Lucie, and told her that her father was assisted by the people, and gone in search of her husband. He found her child and Miss Pross with her; but, it never occurred to him to be surprised by their appearance until a long time afterwards, when he sat watching them in such quiet as the night knew.

---

14 · THE SHADOW

ONE of the first considerations which arose in the business mind of Mr. Lorry when business hours came round, was this:—that he had no right to imperil Tellson's by sheltering the wife of an emigrant prisoner under the Bank roof. His own possessions, safety, life, he would have hazarded for Lucie and her child, without a moment's demur; but the great trust he held was not his own.

Noon coming, and the Doctor not returning, and every minute's delay tending to compromise Tellson's, Mr. Lorry advised with Lucie. She said that her father had spoken of hiring a lodging for a short term, in that Quarter, near the Banking-house. As there was no business objection to this, and as he foresaw that even if it were all well with Charles, and he were to be released, he could not hope to leave the city, Mr. Lorry went out in quest of such a lodging, and found a suitable one, high up in a removed by-street.

To this lodging he at once removed Lucie and her child, and Miss Pross: giving them what comfort he could, and much more than he had himself. He left Jerry with them, as a figure to fill a doorway that would bear considerable knocking on the head, and returned to his own occupations. A disturbed mind he brought to bear upon them, and slowly and heavily the day lagged on with him.

It wore itself out, and wore him out with it, until the Bank closed. He was again alone in his room of the previous night, considering what to do next, when he heard a foot upon the stair. In a few moments a man stood in his presence, who, with a keenly observant look at him, addressed him by his name.

'Your servant,' said Mr. Lorry. 'Do you know me?'

He was a strongly made man with dark curling hair, from forty-five to fifty years of age. For answer he repeated, without any change of emphasis, the words:

'Do you know me?'

'I have seen you somewhere.'

'Perhaps at my wine-shop?'

Much interested and agitated, Mr. Lorry said: 'You come from Doctor Manette?'

'Yes. I come from Doctor Manette.'

'And what says he? What does he send me?'

Defarge gave into his anxious hand, an open scrap of paper. It bore the words in the Doctor's writing:

> 'Charles is safe, but I cannot safely leave this place yet. I have obtained the favour that the bearer has a short note from Charles to his wife. Let the bearer see his wife.'

'Will you accompany me,' said Mr. Lorry, joyfully relieved after reading this note aloud, 'to where his wife resides?'

'Yes,' returned Defarge.

Scarcely noticing as yet, in what a curiously reserved and mechanical way Defarge spoke, Mr. Lorry put on his hat and they went down into the court-yard. There, they found two women; one, knitting.

'Madame Defarge, surely!' said Mr. Lorry, who had left her in exactly the same attitude some seventeen years ago.

'It is she,' observed her husband.

'Does madame go with us?' inquired Mr. Lorry, seeing that she moved as they moved.

'Yes. That she may be able to recognize the faces and know the persons. It is for their safety.'

Beginning to be struck by Defarge's manner, Mr. Lorry looked dubiously at him, and led the way. Both the women followed; the second woman was named The Vengeance.

They passed through the intervening streets as quickly as they might, ascended the staircase of the new domicile, were admitted by Jerry, and found Lucie weeping alone. She was thrown into a transport by the tidings Mr. Lorry gave her of her husband, and clasped the hand that delivered his note—little thinking what it had been doing near him in the night, and might, but for a chance, have done to him.

> 'DEAREST,—Take courage. I am well, and your father has influence around me. You cannot answer this. Kiss our child for me.'

That was all the writing. It was so much, however, to her who received it, that she turned from Defarge to his wife, and kissed one of the hands that knitted. It was a passionate, loving, thankful, womanly action, but the hand made no response—dropped cold and heavy, and took to its knitting again.

There was something in its touch that gave Lucie a check. She stopped in the act of putting the note in her bosom, and, with her hands yet at her neck, looked terrified at Madame Defarge. Madame Defarge met the lifted eyebrows and forehead with a cold, impassive stare.

'My dear,' said Mr. Lorry, striking in to explain; 'there are frequent risings in the streets; and, although it is not likely they will ever trouble you, Madame Defarge wishes to see those whom she has the power to protect at such times, to the end that she may know them—that she may identify them. I believe,' said Mr. Lorry, rather halting in his reassuring words, as the stony manner of all the three impressed itself upon him more and more, 'I state the case, Citizen Defarge?'

Defarge looked gloomily at his wife, and gave no other answer than a gruff sound of acquiescence.

'You had better, Lucie,' said Mr. Lorry, doing all he could to propitiate, by tone and manner, 'have the dear child here, and our good Pross. Our good Pross, Defarge, is an English lady, and knows no French.'

The lady in question, whose rooted conviction that she was more than a match for any foreigner, was not to be shaken by distress and danger, appeared with folded arms, and observed in English to The Vengeance, whom her eyes first encountered, 'Well, I am sure, Boldface! I hope *you* are well!' She also bestowed a British cough on Madame Defarge; but, neither of the two took much heed of her.

'Is that his child?' said Madame Defarge, stopping in her work for the first time, and pointing her knitting-needle at little Lucie as if it were the finger of Fate.

'Yes, madame,' answered Mr. Lorry; 'this is our poor prisoner's daughter, and only child.'

The shadow attendant on Madame Defarge and her party seemed to fall, threatening and dark, on both the mother and the child.

'It is enough, my husband,' said Madame Defarge. 'I have seen them. We may go.'

She resumed her knitting and went out. The Vengeance followed. Defarge went last, and closed the door.

'Courage, my dear Lucie,' said Mr. Lorry. 'Courage,

courage! So far all goes well with us—much, much better than it has of late gone with many poor souls. Cheer up, and have a thankful heart.'

'I am not thankless, I hope, but that dreadful woman seems to throw a shadow on me and on all my hopes.'

'Tut, tut!' said Mr. Lorry; 'what is this despondency? A shadow indeed! No substance in it, Lucie.'

But the shadow of the manner of these Defarges was dark upon himself, for all that, and in his secret mind it troubled him greatly.

Doctor Manette did not return until the morning of the fourth day of his absence. So much of what had happened in that dreadful time as could be kept from the knowledge of Lucie was so well concealed from her, that not until long afterwards, when France and she were far apart, did she know that eleven hundred defenceless prisoners of both sexes and all ages had been killed by the populace. She only knew that there had been an attack upon the prisons, that all political prisoners had been in danger, and that some had been dragged out by the crowd and murdered.

To Mr. Lorry, the Doctor explained, that the crowd had taken him through a scene of carnage to the prison. That, there he had found a self-appointed tribunal sitting. That, he had announced himself by name and profession as having been for eighteen years a secret and unaccused prisoner in the Bastille; that one of the tribunal had risen and identified him, and that this man was Defarge. That, he had learnt that his son-in-law was among the living prisoners, and had pleaded hard to the tribunal for his life and liberty. That, in the first frantic greetings lavished on himself as a notable sufferer under the over-thrown system, it had been accorded to him to have Charles Darnay brought before the lawless Court, and examined. That, he seemed on the point of being at once released, when the tide in his favour met with some unexplained check (not intelligible to the Doctor), which led to a few words of secret conference. That, the man sitting as President had then informed Doctor Manette that the prisoner must remain in custody, but should, for his sake, be held inviolate in safe custody. That, immediately, on a signal, the prisoner was removed to the interior of the prison again; but, that he, the Doctor, had then strongly pleaded for permission to remain and assure himself that his son-in-law was safe. That he had obtained the permission, and had remained until the danger was over.

Greater things than the Doctor had at that time to contend with, would have yielded before his persevering purpose. While he kept himself in his place, as a physician, whose business was with all degrees of mankind, bond and free, rich and poor, bad and good, he used his personal influence so wisely, that he was soon the inspecting physician of three prisons, and among them of La Force. He could now assure Lucie that her husband was no longer confined alone, but was mixed with the general body of prisoners; he saw her husband weekly, and brought sweet messages to her, straight from his lips; sometimes her husband himself sent a letter to her (though never by the Doctor's hand), but she was not permitted to write to him; for, among the many wild suspicions of plots in the prisons, the wildest of all pointed at emigrants who were known to have made friends or permanent connections abroad.

But, though the Doctor tried hard, and never ceased trying, to get Charles Darnay set at liberty, or at least to get him brought to trial, the public current of the time set too strong and fast for him. The new era began; the king was tried, doomed, and beheaded; the Republic of Liberty, Equality, Fraternity, or Death, declared for victory or death against the world in arms; the black flag waved night and day from the great towers of Notre-Dame; three hundred thousand men, summoned to rise against the tyrants of the earth, rose from all the varying soils of France. What private solicitude could rear itself against the deluge of the Year One of Liberty—the deluge rising from below, not falling from above, and with the windows of Heaven shut, not opened!

One hideous figure grew as familiar as if it had been before the general gaze from the foundations of the world—the figure of the sharp female called La Guillotine.

It was the popular theme for jests: it was the best cure for headache; it infallibly prevented the hair from turning grey; it imparted a peculiar delicacy to the complexion; it was the National Razor which shaved close; who kissed La Guillotine, looked through a little window and sneezed into the sack.

Among these terrors, and the brood belonging to them, the Doctor walked with a steady head: confident in his power, never doubting that he would save Lucie's husband at last. Yet the current of the time swept by, so strong and deep, and carried the time away so fiercely, that Charles had lain in prison one year and three months when the Doctor was thus steady and confident. So much more wicked and distracted had the Revolution grown in that December month, that the rivers of the South were encumbered with the bodies of the violently drowned by night, and prisoners were shot in lines and squares under the southern wintry sun. Still, the Doctor walked among the terrors with a steady head. No man better known than he, in Paris at that day; no man in a stranger situation. Silent, humane, indispensable in hospital and prison, using his art equally among assassins and victims, he was a man apart. He was not suspected or brought in question, any more than if he had indeed been recalled to life.

One year and three months. During all that time Lucie was never sure, from hour to hour, but that the Guillotine would strike off her husband's head next day. Every day, through the stony streets, the tumbrils now jolted heavily, filled with Condemned. Lovely girls; bright women, brown-haired, black-haired, and grey; youths; stalwart men and old; gentle born and peasant born; all red wine for La Guillotine, all daily brought into light from the dark cellars of the loathsome prisons, and carried to her through the street to slake her devouring thirst. Liberty, Equality, Fraternity, or Death:—the last, much the easiest to bestow, O Guillotine!

If the suddenness of her calamity, and the whirling wheels of the time, had stunned the Doctor's daughter into awaiting the result in idle despair, it would but have been with her as it was with many. But, from the hour when she had taken the white head to her fresh young bosom in the garret of Saint Antoine, she had been true to her duties.

She did not greatly alter in appearance. She lost her colour, and the old intent expression was a constant, not an occasional, thing; otherwise, she remained very pretty and comely. Sometimes, at night on kissing her father, she would burst into the grief she had repressed all day, and would say that her sole reliance, under Heaven, was on him. He always resolutely answered: 'Nothing can happen to him without my knowledge, and I know that I can save him, Lucie.'

They had not made the round of their changed life many weeks, when her father said to her, on coming home one evening:

'My dear, there is an upper window in the prison, to which Charles can sometimes gain access at three in the afternoon. When he can get to it—which depends on many uncertainties and incidents—he might see you in the street, he thinks, if you stood in a certain place that I can show you. But you will not be able to see him, my poor child, and even if you could, it would be unsafe for you to make a sign of recognition.'

'O show me the place, my father, and I will go there every day.'

From that time, in all weathers, she waited there two hours. As the clock struck two, she was there, and at four she turned resignedly away. When it was not too wet or inclement for her child to be with her, they went together; at other times she was alone; but she never missed a single day.

It was the dark and dirty corner of a small winding street. The hovel of a cutter of wood into lengths for burning, was the only house at that end. On the third day of her being there, he noticed her.

'Good day, citizeness.'

'Good day, citizen.'

This mode of address was now prescribed by decree.

'Walking here again, citizeness?'

'You see me, citizen!'

The wood-sawyer, who was a little man with many gestures (he had once been a mender of roads), pointed at the prison, and putting his ten fingers before his face to represent bars, peeped through them jocosely.

'But it's not my business,' said he. And went on sawing his wood.

In all weathers, in the snow and frost of winter, in the bitter winds of spring, in the hot sunshine of summer, in the rains of autumn, and again in the snow and frost of winter, Lucie passed two hours of every day at this place. Her husband saw her (so she learned from her father) it might be once in five or six times: it might be twice or thrice running: it might be, not for a week or a fortnight together. It was enough that he could and did see her when the chances served.

These occupations brought her round to the December month. On a lightly-snowing afternoon she arrived at the usual corner. It was a day of some wild rejoicing, and a festival. She had seen the houses, as she came along, decorated with little pikes, and with little red caps stuck upon them; also, with tricoloured ribbons; also, with the standard inscription: Republic One and Indivisible. Liberty, Equality, Fraternity, or Death!

The miserable shop of the wood-sawyer was shut and he was not there, which was a relief to Lucie, and left her quite alone.

But, he was not far off, for presently she heard a troubled movement and a shouting coming along, which filled her with fear. A moment afterwards, and a throng of people came pouring round the corner by the prison wall, in the midst of whom was the wood-sawyer hand in hand with The Vengeance. There could not be fewer than five hundred people, and they were dancing like five thousand demons. There was no other music than their own singing. They danced to the popular Revolution song, keeping a ferocious time that was like a gnashing of teeth in unison. At first, they were a mere storm of coarse red caps and coarse woollen rags; but, as they filled the place, and stopped to dance about Lucie, some ghastly apparition of a dance-figure gone raving mad arose among them. They advanced, retreated, struck at one another's hands, clutched at one another's heads, spun round alone, caught one another and spun round in pairs, until many of them dropped. While those were down, the rest linked hand in hand, and all spun round together: then the ring broke, and in separate rings of two and four they turned and turned until they all stopped at once, began again, struck, clutched, and tore, and then reversed the spin, and all spun round another way. Suddenly they stopped again, paused, struck out the time afresh, formed into lines the width of the public way, and, with their heads low down and their hands high up, swooped screaming off.

This was the Carmagnole. As it passed, leaving Lucie frightened and bewildered in the doorway of the wood-sawyer's house, the feathery snow fell as quietly and lay as white and soft, as if it had never been.

'O my father!' for he stood before her when she lifted up the eyes she had momentarily darkened with her hand; 'such a cruel, bad sight.'

'I know, my dear, I know. I have seen it many times. Don't be frightened! Not one of them would harm you.'

'I am not frightened for myself, my father. But when I think of my husband, at the mercies of these people——'

'We will set him above their mercies very soon. I left him climbing to the window, and I came to tell you. There is no one here to see. You may kiss your hand towards that highest shelving roof.'

'I do so, father, and I send him my Soul with it!'

A footstep in the snow. Madame Defarge. 'I salute you,

citizeness,' from the Doctor. 'I salute you, citizen.' This in passing. Nothing more. Madame Defarge gone, like a shadow over the white road.

'Give me your arm, my love. Pass from here with an air of cheerfulness and courage, for his sake. That was well done;' they had left the spot; 'it shall not be in vain. Charles is summoned for to-morrow.'

'For to-morrow!'

'There is no time to lose. I am well prepared, but there are precautions to be taken, that could not be taken until he was actually summoned before the Tribunal. He has not received the notice yet, but I know that he will presently be summoned for to-morrow, and removed to the Conciergerie. You are not afraid?'

She could scarcely answer, 'I trust in you.'

'Do so. Your suspense is nearly ended, my darling; he shall be restored to you within a few hours; I have encompassed him with every protection. I must see Lorry.'

He stopped. There was a heavy lumbering of wheels within hearing. They both knew too well what it meant. One. Two. Three. Three tumbrils faring away with their dread loads over the hushing snow.

'I must see Lorry,' the Doctor repeated, turning her another way.

The staunch old gentleman was still in his trust; had never left it. A murky red and yellow sky, and a rising mist from the Seine, denoted the approach of darkness. It was almost dark when they arrived at the Bank. Who could that be with Mr. Lorry—the owner of the riding-coat upon the chair—who must not be seen? From whom newly arrived, did he come out, agitated and surprised, to take his favourite in his arms? To whom did he appear to repeat her faltering words, when, raising his voice and turning his head towards the door of the room from which he had issued, he said: 'Removed to the Conciergerie, and summoned for to-morrow'?

---

15 · TRIUMPH

The dread Tribunal of five Judges, Public Prosecutor, and determined Jury, sat every day. Their lists went forth every evening, and were read out by the gaolers of the various prisons to their prisoners. The standard gaoler-joke was, 'Come out and listen to the Evening Paper, you inside there!'

'Charles Evrémonde, called Darnay!'

So at last began the Evening Paper at La Force.

The passage to the Conciergerie was short and dark; the night in its vermin-haunted cells was long and cold. Next day, fifteen prisoners were put to the bar before Charles Darnay's name was called. All the fifteen were condemned, and the trials of the whole occupied an hour and a half.

'Charles Evrémonde, called Darnay,' was at length arraigned.

His judges sat upon the Bench in feathered hats; but the rough red cap and tricoloured cockade was the head-dress otherwise prevailing. Looking at the Jury and the turbulent audience, he might have thought that the usual order of things was reversed, and that the felons were trying the honest men. The lowest, cruelest, and worst populace of the city were there, noisily commenting, applauding, disapproving, anticipating, and precipitating the result, without a check. Of the men, the greater part were armed in various ways; of the women, some wore knives, some daggers, some ate and drank as they looked on, many knitted. Among these last, was one, with a spare piece of knitting under her arm as she worked. She was in a front row, by the side of a man whom he had never seen since his arrival at the Barrier, but whom he directly remembered as Defarge. What he most noticed in the two figures was, that although they were posted as close to himself as they could be, they never looked towards him. They seemed to be waiting for something with a dogged determination, and they looked at the Jury, but at nothing else. Under the President sat Doctor Manette, in his usual quiet dress. As well as the prisoner could see, he and Mr. Lorry were the only men there who wore their usual clothes, and had not assumed the coarse garb of the Carmagnole.

Charles Evrémonde, called Darnay, was accused by the public prosecutor as an emigrant, whose life was forfeit to the Republic, under the decree which banished all emigrants on pain of Death. It was nothing that the decree bore date since his return to France. There he was, and there was the decree; he had been taken in France, and his head was demanded.

'Take off his head!' cried the audience. 'An enemy to the Republic!'

The President rang his bell to silence those cries, and asked the prisoner whether it was not true that he had lived many years in England?

Undoubtedly it was.

Was he not an emigrant then? What did he call himself?

Not an emigrant, he hoped, within the sense and spirit of the law.

Why not? the President desired to know.

Because he had voluntarily relinquished a title that was distasteful to him, and had left his country—he submitted before the word emigrant in the present acceptation by the

Tribunal was in use—to live by his own industry in England, rather than on the industry of the overladen people of France.

What proof had he of this?

He handed in the names of two witnesses: Théophile Gabelle, and Alexandre Manette.

But he had married in England? the President reminded him.

True, but not an English woman.

A citizeness of France?

Yes. By birth.

Her name and family?

'Lucie Manette, only daughter of Doctor Manette, the good physician who sits there.'

This answer had a happy effect upon the audience. Cries in exaltation of the well-known good physician rent the hall. So capriciously were the people moved, that tears immediately rolled down several ferocious countenances which had been glaring at the prisoner a moment before.

On these few steps of his dangerous way, Charles Darnay had set his foot according to Doctor Manette's instructions. The same cautious counsel directed every step that lay before him.

The President asked, why had he returned to France when he did, and not sooner?

He had not returned sooner, he replied, simply because he had no means of living in France, save those he had resigned; whereas, in England, he lived by giving instruction in the French language and literature. He had returned when he did, on the pressing and written entreaty of a French citizen, who represented that his life was endangered by his absence. He had come back, to save a citizen's life, and to bear his testimony, at whatever personal hazard, to the truth. Was that criminal in the eyes of the Republic?

The populace cried enthusiastically, 'No!' and the President rang his bell to quiet them. Which it did not, for they continued to cry 'No!' until they left off, of their own will.

The President required the name of that citizen? The accused explained that the citizen was his first witness. He also referred with confidence to the citizen's letter, which had been taken from him at the Barrier, but which he did not doubt would be found among the papers then before the President.

The Doctor had taken care that it should be there, and it was produced and read. Citizen Gabelle was called to confirm it, and did so. Citizen Gabelle hinted, with infinite delicacy and politeness, that in the pressure of business imposed on the Tribunal, he had been slightly overlooked in his prison of the Abbaye, until three days ago, when he had been set at liberty.

Doctor Manette was next questioned. His high personal popularity, and the clearness of his answers, made a great impression; but, as he proceeded, as he showed that the Accused was his first friend on his release from his long imprisonment; that, the Accused had remained in England always faithful and devoted to his daughter and himself in their exile; that, so far from being in favour with the Aristocrat government there, he had actually been tried for his life by it, as the foe of England and friend of the United States—as he brought these circumstances into view, with the greatest discretion and with the straightforward force of truth and earnestness, the Jury and the populace became one. The Jury declared that they had heard enough, and that they were ready with their votes if the President were content to receive them.

At every vote (the Jurymen voted aloud and individually), the populace set up a shout of applause. All the voices were in the prisoner's favour, and the President declared him free.

Then, began one of those extraordinary scenes with which the populace sometimes gratified their fickleness, or their better impulses towards generosity and mercy, or which they regarded as some set-off against their swollen account of cruel rage.

When he and Doctor Manette emerged from the gate, there was a great crowd about it, in which there seemed to be every face he had seen in court—except two. They put him into a great chair they had taken out of the court itself. In this car of triumph, he was carried to his home.

As he held Lucie to his heart and their lips came together, a few of the people fell to dancing. Instantly, all the rest fell to dancing, and the court-yard overflowed with the Carmagnole. Then, they elevated into the vacant chair a young woman from the crowd to be carried as the Goddess of Liberty, and then swelling and overflowing out into the adjacent streets, and along the river's bank, and over the bridge, the Carmagnole absorbed them every one and whirled them away.

---

16 · A KNOCK AT THE DOOR

IN the universal fear and distrust that darkened the time, all the usual harmless ways of life were changed. In the Doctor's little household, as in very many others, the articles of daily consumption that were wanted were purchased every evening, in small quantities and at various small shops. For some months past, Miss Pross and Mr. Cruncher had discharged the office of purveyors; the former carrying the money; the latter, the basket. Every afternoon at about the time when the public lamps were lighted, they fared forth on this duty, and made and brought home such purchases as were needful.

This time arrived shortly after the triumphant return of Charles and Doctor Manette.

'Now, Mr. Cruncher,' said Miss Pross, whose eyes were red with felicity; 'if you are ready, I am.'

Jerry hoarsely professed himself at Miss Pross's service. They went out, leaving Lucie, and her husband, her father, and the child, by a bright fire. Mr. Lorry was expected back presently from the Banking House. Miss Pross had lighted the lamp, but had put it aside in a corner, that they might enjoy the fire-light undisturbed.

All was subdued and quiet, and Lucie was more at ease than she had been.

'What is that?' she cried, all at once.

'My dear!' said her father, laying his hand on hers, 'command yourself. What a disordered state you are in!'

'I thought, my father,' said Lucie, excusing herself, with a pale face and in a faltering voice, 'that I heard strange feet upon the stairs.'

'My love, the staircase is as still as Death.'

As he said the word, a blow was struck upon the door.

'Oh father, father. What can this be! Hide Charles. Save him!'

'My child,' said the Doctor rising, and laying his hand upon her shoulder, 'I *have* saved him. What weakness is this, my dear! Let me go to the door.'

He took the lamp in his hand, crossed the two intervening outer rooms, and opened it. A rude clattering of feet over the floor, and four rough men in red caps, armed with sabres and pistols, entered the room.

'The Citizen Evrémonde, called Darnay,' said the first.

'Who seeks him?' answered Darnay.

'I seek him. We seek him. I know you, Evrémonde; I saw you before the Tribunal to-day. You are again the prisoner of the Republic.'

The four surrounded him, where he stood with his wife and child clinging to him.

'Tell me how and why am I again a prisoner?'

'It is enough that you return straight to the Conciergerie, and will know to-morrow. You are summoned for to-morrow.'

Dr. Manette, whom this visitation had so turned into stone, that he stood with the lamp in his hand, as if he were a statue made to hold it, moved after these words were spoken, put the lamp down, and confronting the speaker, said:

'You know him, you have said. Do you know me?'

'Yes, I know you, Citizen Doctor.'

'We all know you, Citizen Doctor,' said the other three.

He looked abstractedly from one to another, and said, in a lower voice, after a pause:

'Will you answer his question to me then? How does this happen?'

'Citizen Doctor,' said the first, reluctantly, 'he has been denounced to the Section of Saint Antoine. This citizen,' pointing out the second who had entered, 'is from Saint Antoine.'

The citizen here indicated nodded his head, and added:

'He is accused by Saint Antoine.'

'Of what?' asked the Doctor.

'Citizen Doctor,' said the first, with his former reluctance, 'ask no more. If the Republic demands sacrifices from you, without doubt you as a good patriot will be happy to make them. Evrémonde, we are pressed.'

'One word,' the Doctor entreated. 'Will you tell me who denounced him?'

'It is against rule,' answered the first; 'but you can ask Him of Saint Antoine here.'

The Doctor turned his eyes upon that man. Who moved uneasily on his feet, rubbed his beard a little, and at length said:

'Well! Truly it is against rule. But he is denounced—and gravely—by the Citizen and Citizeness Defarge. And by one other.'

'What other?'

'Do *you* ask, Citizen Doctor?'

'Yes.'

'Then,' said he of Saint Antoine, with a strange look, 'you will be answered to-morrow. Now, I am dumb!'

Mr. Lorry had just finished his dinner, and was sitting before a cheery little log or two of fire—perhaps looking into their blaze for the picture of that younger elderly gentleman from Tellson's, who had looked into the red coals at the Royal George at Dover, now a good many years ago. He turned his head as Sydney Carton entered, and showed the surprise with which he also saw a stranger.

'Good evening, sir,' said Sydney. 'Mr. Barsad.'

'Barsad?' repeated the old gentleman, 'Barsad? I have an association with the name—and with the face.'

'I told you you had a remarkable face, Mr. Barsad,' observed Carton, coolly. 'Pray sit down.'

As he took a chair himself, he supplied the link that Mr. Lorry wanted, by saying to him with a frown, 'Witness at that trial.' Mr. Lorry immediately remembered, and regarded his new visitor with an undisguised look of abhorrence.

'Mr. Barsad has been persuaded by me to come here to discuss a matter of business,' said Sydney. 'I have bad news. Darnay has been arrested again.'

Struck with consternation, the old gentleman exclaimed, 'What do you tell me! I left him safe and free within these two hours, and am about to return to him!'

'Arrested for all that. When was it done, Mr. Barsad?'

'Just now.'

'Mr. Barsad is the best authority possible, sir,' said Sydney, 'and I have it from Mr. Barsad's communication to a friend and brother spy, over a bottle of wine, that the arrest has taken place. He left the messengers at the gate and saw them admitted by the porter. There is no doubt that he is retaken.'

Mr. Lorry's business eye read in the speaker's face that it was loss of time to dwell upon the point. Confused, but sensible that something might depend on his presence of mind, he commanded himself, and was silently attentive.

'Now, I trust,' said Sydney to him, 'that the name and influence of Doctor Manette may stand him in as good stead to-morrow—you said he would be before the Tribunal again to-morrow, Mr. Barsad?——'

'Yes; I believe so.'

'—in as good stead to-morrow as to-day. But it may not be so. I own to you, I am shaken, Mr. Lorry, by Doctor Manette's not having had the power to prevent this arrest.'

'He may not have known of it beforehand,' said Mr. Lorry.

'But that very circumstance would be alarming, when we remember how identified he is with his son-in-law.'

'That's true,' Mr. Lorry acknowledged, with his troubled hand at his chin, and his troubled eyes on Carton.

'In short,' said Sydney, 'this is a desperate time, when desperate games are played for desperate stakes. Let the Doctor play the winning game; I will play the losing one. No man's life here is worth purchase. Anyone carried home by the people to-day, may be condemned to-morrow. Now, the stake I have resolved to play for, in case of the worst, is a friend in the Conciergerie. And the friend I purpose to myself to win, is Mr. Barsad.'

'You need have good cards, sir,' said the spy.

'I'll run them over. I'll see what I hold.—Mr. Lorry, you know what a brute I am; I wish you'd give me a little brandy.'

It was put before him, and he drank off a glassful—drank off another glassful—pushed the bottle thoughtfully away.

'Mr. Barsad,' he went on, in the tone of one who really was looking over a hand at cards: 'Sheep of the prisons, emissary of Republican committees, now turnkey, now prisoner, always spy and secret informer. Mr. Barsad, now in the employ of the republican French government, was formerly in the employ of the aristocratic English government, the enemy of France and freedom. That's an excellent card. Inference clear as day in this region of suspicion, that Mr. Barsad, still in the pay of the aristocatic English government, is the spy of Pitt, the treacherous foe of the Republic crouching in its bosom, the English traitor and agent of all mischief so much spoken of and so difficult to find. That's a card not to be beaten. Have you followed my hand, Mr. Barsad?'

'Not to understand your play,' returned the spy, somewhat uneasily.

'I play my Ace, Denunciation of Mr. Barsad to the nearest Section Committee. Look over your hand, Mr. Barsad, and see what you have. Don't hurry.'

He drew the bottle near, poured out another glassful of brandy, and drank it off. He saw that the spy was fearful of his drinking himself into a fit state for the immediate denunciation of him. Seeing it, he poured out and drank another glassful.

'Look over your hand carefully, Mr. Barsad. Take time.'

It was a poorer hand than he suspected. Mr. Barsad saw losing cards in it that Sydney Carton knew nothing of. Thrown out of his employment in England, through too much unsuccessful hard swearing there, he knew that he had crossed the Channel, and accepted service in France: first, as a tempter and an eavesdropper among his own countrymen there: gradually, as a tempter and an eavesdropper among the natives. He knew that under the overthrown government he had been a spy upon Saint Antoine and Defarge's wine-shop. He always remembered with fear and trembling, that that terrible woman had knitted when he talked with her, and had looked ominously at him as her fingers moved. He had since seen her, in the Section of Saint Antoine, over and over again produce her knitted registers, and denounce people whose lives the guillotine then surely swallowed up. He knew, as everyone employed as he was did, that he was never safe; that flight was impossible; that he was tied fast under the shadow of the axe; and that a word might bring it down upon him. Once denounced, and on such grave grounds as had just now been suggested to his mind, he foresaw that the dreadful woman of whose unrelenting character he had seen many proofs, would produce against him that fatal register, and would quash his last chance of life. Here were surely cards enough of one black suit, to justify the holder in growing rather livid as he turned them over.

'You scarcely seem to like your hand,' said Sydney, with the greatest composure. 'Do you play?'

The spy turned to him, and said, with desperation, 'It has come to a point. I go on duty soon, and can't overstay my time. You told me you had a proposal; what is it? Now, it is of no use asking too much of me. Ask me to do anything putting my head in great extra danger, and I had better trust my life to the chances of a refusal than the chances of consent. In short, I should make that choice. You talk of desperation. We are all desperate here. Remember! I may denounce you if I think proper, and I can swear my way through stone walls, and so can others. Now, what do you want with me?'

'Not very much. You are a turnkey at the Conciergerie?'

'I tell you once for all, there is no such thing as an escape possible,' said the spy, firmly.

'Why need you tell me what I have not asked? You are a turnkey at the Conciergerie?'

'I am sometimes.'

'You can be when you choose?'

'I can pass in and out when I choose.'

Sydney Carton filled another glass with brandy, poured it slowly out upon the hearth, and watched it as it dropped. It being all spent, he said, rising:

'So far, we have spoken before Mr. Lorry, because it was as well that the merits of the cards should not rest solely between you and me. Come into the dark room here, and let us have one final word alone.'

---

17 · THE SHADOW DEEPENS

MR. LORRY was still sitting in worried thought by the fire, as Sydney Carton and the spy returned from the dark room. 'Adieu, Mr. Barsad,' said the former; 'our arrangement thus made, you have nothing to fear from me.'

He sat down in a chair on the hearth, over against Mr. Lorry. When they were alone, Mr. Lorry asked him what he had done?

'Not much. If it should go ill with the prisoner, I have ensured access to him, once.'

Mr. Lorry's countenance fell.

'It is all I could do.' said Carton. 'To propose too much, would be to put this man's head under the axe, and, as he himself said, nothing worse could happen to him if he were denounced.'

'But access to him,' said Mr. Lorry, 'if it should go ill before the Tribunal, will not save him.'

'I never said it would.'

Mr. Lorry's eyes gradually sought the fire; his sympathy with his darling, and the heavy disappointment of this second arrest, gradually weakened them; he was an old man now, overborne with anxiety of late, and his tears fell.

'You are a good man and true friend,' said Carton, in an altered voice. 'Forgive me if I notice that you are affected. I could not see my father weep, and sit by, careless. And I could not respect your sorrow more, if you were my father. You are free from that misfortune, however.'

Though he said the last words with a slip into his usual manner, there was a true feeling and respect both in his tone and in his touch, that Mr. Lorry, who had never seen the better side of him, was wholly unprepared for. He gave him his hand, and Carton gently pressed it.

'To return to poor Darnay,' said Carton. 'Don't tell Her of this interview, or this arrangement. It would not enable her to go to see him. Don't speak of me to her. As I said to you when I first came, I had better not see her. I can put my hand out, to do any little helpful work for her that my hand can find to do, without that. You are going to her, I hope? She must be very desolate to-night.'

'I am going now, directly.'

'I am glad of that. She has such a strong attachment to you and reliance on you. How does she look?'

'Anxious and unhappy, but very beautiful.'

'Ah!'

It was a long, grieving sound, like a sigh—almost like a sob. It attracted Mr. Lorry's eyes to Carton's face, which was turned to the fire. He wore the white riding-coat and top-boots, then in vogue, and the light of the fire touching their light surfaces made him look very pale, with his long brown hair, all untrimmed, hanging loose about him.

'And your duties here have drawn to an end, sir?' said Carton, turning to him.

'Yes. As I was telling you last night when Lucie came in so unexpectedly, I have at length done all that I can do here. I hoped to have left them in perfect safety, and then to have quitted Paris. I have my Leave to Pass. I was ready to go.'

They were both silent.

'Yours is a long life to look back upon, sir?' said Carton, wistfully.

'I am in my seventy-eighth year.'

'You have been useful all your life; steadily and constantly occupied; trusted, respected, and looked up to?'

'I have been a man of business, ever since I have been a man.'

'See what a place you fill at seventy-eight. How many people will miss you when you leave it empty!'

'A solitary old bachelor,' answered Mr. Lorry, shaking his head. 'There is nobody to weep for me.'

'How can you say that? Wouldn't She weep for you? Wouldn't her child?'

'Yes, yes, thank God. I didn't quite mean what I said.'

'It *is* a thing to thank God for; is it not?'

'Surely, surely.'

'If you could say, with truth, to your own solitary heart, to-night, "I have secured to myself the love and attachment, the gratitude or respect, of no human creature; I have won myself a tender place in no regard; I have done nothing good or serviceable to be remembered by!" your seventy-eight years would be seventy-eight heavy curses; would they not?'

'You say truly, Mr. Carton; I think they would be.'

'I'll walk with you to her gate. You know my vagabond and restless habits. If I should prowl about the streets a long time, don't be uneasy; I shall reappear in the morning. You go to the court to-morrow?'

'Yes, unhappily.'

'I shall be there, but only as one of the crowd. My Spy will find a place for me. Take my arm, sir.'

Mr. Lorry did so, and they went down-stairs and out in the

streets. A few minutes brought them to Mr. Lorry's destination. Carton left him there; but lingered at a little distance, and turned back to the gate again when it was shut, and touched it. He had heard of her going to the prison every day. 'She came out here,' he said, looking about him, 'turned this way, must have trod on these stones often. Let me follow in her steps.'

It was ten o'clock at night when he stood before the prison of La Force, where she had stood hundreds of times. A little wood-sawyer, having closed his shop, was smoking his pipe at his shop-door.

'Good-night, citizen,' said Sydney Carton, pausing in going by; for, the man eyed him inquisitively.

'Good-night, citizen.'

'How goes the Republic?'

'You mean the Guillotine. Not ill. Sixty-three to-day. We shall mount to a hundred soon. Samson and his men complain sometimes, of being exhausted. Ha, ha, ha! He is so droll, that Samson. Such a Barber!'

'Do you often go to see him——'

'Shave? Always. Every day. What a barber! You have seen him at work?'

'Never.'

'Go and see him when he has a good batch. Figure this to yourself, citizen; he shaved the sixty-three to-day, in less than two pipes! Less than two pipes. Word of honour!', and the grinning little man held out the pipe he was smoking, to explain how he timed the executioner.

'But you are not English,' said the wood-sawyer, 'though you wear English dress?'

'Yes,' said Carton, pausing again, and answering over his shoulder.

'You speak like a Frenchman.'

'I am an old student here.'

'Aha, a perfect Frenchman! Good-night, Englishman.'

'Good-night, citizen!'

Sydney had not gone far out of sight, when he stopped in the middle of the street under a glimmering lamp, and wrote with his pencil on a scrap of paper. Then, traversing with the decided step of one who remembered the way well, several dark and dirty streets, he stopped at a chemist's shop, which the owner was closing with his own hands. Giving this citizen, too, good-night, as he confronted him at his counter, he laid the scrap of paper before him. 'Whew!' the chemist whistled softly, as he read it. 'Hi! hi! hi!'

Sydney Carton took no heed, and the chemist said:

'For you, citizen?'

'For me.'

'You will be careful to keep them separate, citizen? You know the consequences of mixing them?'

'Perfectly.'

Certain small packets were made and given to him. He put them, one by one, in the breast of his inner coat, counted out the money for them, and deliberately left the shop. 'There is nothing more to do,' said he, glancing upward at the moon, 'until to-morrow. I can't sleep.'

It was not a reckless manner, the manner in which he said these words aloud under the fast-sailing clouds, nor was it more expressive of negligence than defiance. It was the settled manner of a tired man, who had wandered and struggled and got lost, but who at length struck into his road and saw its end.

Long ago, when he had been famous among his earliest competitors as a youth of great promise, he had followed his father to the grave. His mother had died, years before. These solemn words, which had been read at his father's grave, arose in his mind as he went down the dark streets, among the heavy shadows, with the moon and the clouds sailing on high above him. 'I am the resurrection and the life, saith the Lord: he that believeth in me, though he were dead, yet shall he live: and whosoever liveth and believeth in me, shall never die.'

The night wore out, and, as he stood upon the bridge listening to the water as it splashed the river walls of the Island of Paris, the day came coldly.

Mr. Lorry was already out when he got back, and it was easy to surmise where the good old man was gone. Sydney Carton drank nothing but a little coffee, ate some bread, and went out to the place of trial.

The court was all astir and a-buzz when the black sheep—whom many fell away from in dread—pressed him into a seat in a corner. Mr. Lorry was there, and Doctor Manette was there. She was there, sitting beside her father. When her husband was brought in, she turned a look upon him, encouraging, full of admiring love and tenderness, all pity, yet courageous for his sake.

Every eye was turned to the jury. The same determined patriots and good republicans as yesterday and the day before, and to-morrow and the day after. No pity there. Every eye then turned to the five judges and the public prosecutor. No favourable leaning in that quarter to-day. A murderous business-meaning there.

Charles Evrémonde, called Darnay. Released yesterday. Re-accused and retaken yesterday. Indictment delivered to him last night. Suspected and denounced enemy of the Republic. Aristocrat, one of a family of tyrants, one of a race proscribed, for that they had used their abolished privileges to the infamous oppression of the people. Charles Evrémonde, called Darnay, in right of such proscription, absolutely Dead in Law.

To this effect, in as few or fewer words, the Public Prosecutor.

The President asked, was the Accused openly denounced or secretly?

'Openly, President.'

'By whom?'

'Three voices, Ernest Defarge, wine-vendor of Saint Antoine.'

'Good.'

'Thérèse Defarge, his wife.'

'Good.'

'Alexandre Manette, physician.'

A great uproar took place in the court, and in the midst of it, Doctor Manette was seen, pale and trembling, standing where he had been seated.

'President, this is a forgery and a fraud. You know the accused to be the husband of my daughter. My daughter, and those dear to her, are far dearer to me than my life. Who and where is the false conspirator who says that I denounce the husband of my child!'

'Citizen Manette, be tranquil. To fail in submission to the authority of the Tribunal would be to put yourself out of Law. As to what is dearer to you than life, nothing can be so dear to a good citizen as the Republic.'

Loud acclamations hailed this rebuke. The President rang his bell, and with warmth resumed.

'If the Republic should demand of you the sacrifice of your child herself, you would have no duty but to sacrifice her. Listen to what is to follow. In the meanwhile, be silent!'

Frantic acclamations were again raised. Doctor Manette sat down, with his eyes looking around, and his lips trembling; his daughter drew closer to him.

Defarge was produced, when the court was quiet enough to admit of his being heard, and rapidly expounded the story of the imprisonment, and of his having been a mere boy in the Doctor's service, and of the release, and of the state of the prisoner when released and delivered to him. This short examination followed, for the court was quick with its work.

'You did good service at the taking of the Bastille, citizen?'

'I believe so.'

'Inform the Tribunal of what you did that day within the Bastille, citizen.'

'I knew,' said Defarge, looking down at his wife, who stood at the bottom of the steps on which he was raised, looking steadily up at him; 'I knew that this prisoner, of whom I speak, had been confined in a cell known as One Hundred and Five, North Tower. I knew it from himself. He knew himself by no other name than One Hundred and Five, North Tower, when he made shoes under my care. As I serve my gun that day, I resolve, when the place shall fall, to examine that cell. It falls. I mount to the cell, with a fellow-citizen, directed by a gaoler. I examine it, very closely. In a hole in the chimney, where a stone has been worked out and replaced, I find a written paper. This is that written paper. I have made it my business to examine some specimens of the writing of Doctor Manette. This is the writing of Doctor Manette. I confide this paper, in the writing of Doctor Manette, to the hands of the President.'

'Let it be read.'

In a dead silence and stillness—the prisoner under trial looking lovingly at his wife, his wife only looking from him to look with solicitude at her father, Doctor Manette keeping his eyes fixed on the reader, Madame Defarge never taking hers from the prisoner, Defarge never taking his from his feasting wife, and all the other eyes there intent upon the Doctor, who saw none of them—the paper was read.

---

18 · THE PAPER

'I, Alexandre Manette, unfortunate physician, native of Beauvais, and afterwards resident in Paris, write this in my cell in the Bastille, during the last month of the year 1767. I write it at stolen intervals, under every difficulty. I design to secrete it in the wall of the chimney, where I have slowly and laboriously made a place of concealment for it.

'These words are formed by the rusty iron point with which I write with difficulty in scrapings of soot and charcoal from the chimney, mixed with blood, in the last month of the tenth year of my captivity. Hope has quite departed from my breast. I know from terrible warnings I have noted in myself that my reason will not long remain unimpaired, but I solemnly declare that I am at this time in the possession of my right mind—that my memory is exact and circumstantial—and that I write the truth.

'One cloudy moonlight night, in the third week of December in the year 1757, I was walking by the Seine for the refreshment of the frosty air, at an hour's distance from my place of residence in the Street of the School of Medicine, when a carriage came along behind me, driven very fast.

As I stood aside to let that carriage pass, a head was put out at the window, and a voice called to the driver to stop.

'The carriage stopped as soon as the driver could rein in his horses, and the same voice called to me by my name. I answered. The carriage was then so far in advance of me that two gentlemen had time to open the door and alight before I came up with it. As they stood side by side near the carriage door, I observed that they both looked of about my own age, or rather younger, and that they were greatly alike, in stature, manner, voice, and (as far as I could see) face too.

' "You are Doctor Manette?" said one.

' "I am."

' "Doctor Manette, formerly of Beauvais," said the other; "the young physician, who within the last year or two has made a rising reputation in Paris?"

' "Gentlemen," I returned, "I am that Doctor Manette of whom you speak so graciously."

' "We have been to your residence," said the first, "and not finding you there, and being informed that you were probably walking in this direction, we followed. Will you please to enter the carriage?"

'The manner of both was imperious, and they both moved, as these words were spoken, so as to place me between themselves and the carriage door. They were armed. I was not.

'I could do nothing but comply, and I entered it in silence. They both entered after me—the last springing in, after putting up the steps. The carriage turned about, and drove on at its former speed.

'I repeat this conversation exactly as it occurred. I have no doubt that it is, word for word, the same. I describe everything exactly as it took place, constraining my mind not to wander from the task. Where I make the broken marks that follow here, I leave off for the time, and put my paper in its hiding-place. * * * *

'The carriage left the streets behind, passed the North Barrier, and emerged upon the country road. At some distance from the Barrier, it struck out of the main avenue, and presently stopped at a solitary house. We all three alighted, and walked, by a damp soft path, to the door of the house. It was not opened immediately, in answer to the ringing of the bell, and one of my two conductors struck the man who opened it, with his heavy riding-glove, across the face.

'There was nothing in this action to attract my particular attention, for I had seen common people struck more commonly than dogs. But, the other of the two, being angry likewise, struck the man in like manner with his arm; the look and bearing of the brothers were then so exactly alike, that I then first perceived them to be twin brothers.

'From the time of our alighting at the outer gate, I had heard cries proceeding from an upper chamber. I was conducted to this chamber straight, and I found a patient in a high fever of the brain, lying on a bed.

'The patient was a woman of great beauty, and young; assuredly not much past twenty. Her hair was torn, and her arms were bound to her sides with sashes and handkerchiefs. I noticed that these bonds were all portions of a gentleman's dress. On one of them, which was a fringed scarf for a dress of ceremony, I saw the armorial bearings of a Noble, and the letter E.

'I turned her gently over, and looked into her face. Her eyes were dilated and wild, and she constantly uttered piercing shrieks, and repeated the words, "My husband, my father, and my brother!" and then counted up to twelve, and said "Hush!" For an instant, and no more, she would pause to listen, and then the piercing shrieks would begin again, and she would repeat the cry, "My husband, my father, and my brother!" and would count up to twelve, and say "Hush!" There was no variation in the order, or the manner. There was no cessation, but the regular moment's pause, in the utterance of these sounds.

' "How long," I asked, "has this lasted?"

'To distinguish the brothers, I will call them the elder and the younger; by the elder, I mean him who exercised the most authority. It was the elder who replied, "Since about this hour last night."

' "She has a husband, a father, and a brother?"

' "A brother."

' "She has some recent association with the number twelve?"

'The younger brother impatiently rejoined, "With twelve o'clock!"

' "See, gentlemen," said I, "how useless I am, as you have brought me! If I had known what I was coming to see, I could have come provided. As it is, time must be lost. There are no medicines to be obtained in this lonely place."

'The elder brother looked to the younger, who said haughtily, "There is a case of medicines here"; and brought it from a closet, and put it on the table. * * * *

'I opened some of the bottles, smelt them, and put the stoppers to my lips.

' "Do you doubt them?" asked the younger brother.

' "You see, monsieur, I am going to use them," I replied, and said no more.

'I made the patient swallow, with great difficulty, and after many efforts, the dose that I desired to give. As I intended to repeat it after a while, and as it was necessary to watch its influence, I then sat down by the side of the bed. I had sat there for half an hour, with the two brothers looking on, before the elder said:

' "There is another patient."

'I was startled and asked, "Is it a pressing case?"

' "You had better see," he carelessly answered; and took up a light. * * * *

'The other patient lay in a back room across a second staircase, which was a species of loft over a stable. There was a low plastered ceiling to a part of it; the rest was open, to the ridge of the tiled roof, and there were beams across. Hay and straw were stored in that portion of the place, faggots for firing, and a heap of apples in sand. I had to pass through that part, to get to the other. My memory is circumstantial and unshaken. I try it with these details, and I see them all, in this my cell in the Bastille, near the close of the tenth year of my captivity, as I saw them all that night.

'On some hay on the ground, with a cushion thrown under his head, lay a handsome peasant-boy—a boy of not more than seventeen at the most. He lay on his back, with his teeth set, his right hand clenched over a wound on his breast, and his glaring eyes looking straight upward.

'The wound was a sword-thrust, received from twenty to twenty-four hours before, but no skill could have saved him if it had been looked to without delay. He was then dying fast. As I turned my eyes to the elder brother, I saw him looking down at this handsome boy whose life was ebbing out, as if he were a wounded bird, or hare, or rabbit; not at all as if he were a fellow-creature.

' "How has this been done, monsieur?" said I.

' "A crazed young common dog! A serf! Forced my

brother to draw upon him, and has fallen by my brother's sword—like a gentleman."

'There was no touch of pity, sorrow, or kindred humanity, in this answer. He was quite incapable of any compassionate feeling about the boy, or about his fate.

'The boy's eyes had slowly moved to him as he had spoken, and they now slowly moved to me.

' "Doctor, they are very proud, these Nobles; but we common dogs are proud too, sometimes. They plunder us, outrage us, beat us, kill us; but we have a little pride left, sometimes. She—have you seen her, Doctor?"

'I said, "I have seen her."

' "She is my sister, Doctor. She was a good girl. She was betrothed to a good young man, too: a tenant of his—that man's who stands there. The other is his brother, the worst of a bad race."

'It was with the greatest difficulty that the boy gathered bodily force to speak; but, his spirit spoke with a dreadful emphasis.

' "We were so robbed by that man who stands there, as all we common dogs are by those superior Beings, and were made so poor, that our father told us it was a dreadful thing to bring a child into the world. Nevertheless, Doctor, my sister married. He was ailing at that time, poor fellow, and she married him that she might tend and comfort him in our cottage. She had not been married many weeks, when that man's brother saw her and admired her, and asked that man to lend her to him—for what are husbands among us! But my sister was good and virtuous, and hated his brother with a hatred as strong as mine. What did the two then, to persuade her husband to use his influence with her, to make her willing?

' "You know, Doctor, that it is among the Rights of these Nobles to harness us common dogs to carts, and drive us. They so harnessed him and drove him. You know that it is among their Rights to keep us in their grounds all night, quieting the frogs, in order that their noble sleep may not be disturbed. They kept him out in the unwholesome mists at night, and ordered him back into his harness in the day. But he was not persuaded. No! Taken out of harness one day at noon, to feed—if he could find food—he sobbed twelve times, once for every stroke of the bell, and died on her bosom."

'Nothing human could have held life in the boy but his determination to tell all his wrong.

' "Then, with that man's permission and even with his aid, his brother took her away for his pleasure and diversion, for a little while. I saw her pass me on the road. When I took the tidings home, our father's heart burst; he never spoke one of the words that filled it. I took my young sister (for I have another) to a place beyond the reach of this man, and where, at least, she will never be *his* vassal. Then, I tracked the brother here, and last night climbed in—a common dog, but sword in hand.—Where is the loft window? It was somewhere here?"

'The room was darkening to his sight; the world was narrowing around him. I glanced about me, and saw that the hay and straw were trampled over the floor, as if there had been a struggle.

' "She heard me, and ran in. I told her not to come near us till he was dead. He came in and first tossed me some pieces of money; then struck at me with a whip. But I, though a common dog, so struck at him as to make him draw. Let him break into as many pieces as he will, the sword that he stained with my common blood; he drew to defend himself—thrust at me with all his skill for his life."

'My glance had fallen, but a few moments before, on the fragments of a broken sword, lying among the hay. That weapon was a gentleman's. In another place, lay an old sword that seemed to have been a soldier's.

' "Now lift me up, Doctor; lift me up. Where is he?"

' "He is not here," I said, supporting the boy, and thinking that he referred to the brother.

' "He! Proud as these nobles are, he is afraid to see me. Where is the man who was here? Turn my face to him."

'I did so, raising the boy's head against my knee. But, invested for the moment with extraordinary power, he raised himself completely.

' "Marquis," said the boy, turned to him, "in the days when all these things are to be answered for, I summon you and yours, to the last of your bad race, to answer for them. I mark this cross of blood upon you, as a sign that I do it. In the days when all these things are to be answered for, I summon your brother, the worst of the bad race, to answer for them separately. I mark this cross of blood upon him, as a sign that I do it."

'Twice, he put his hand to the wound in his breast, and with his forefinger drew a cross in the air. He stood for an instant with the finger yet raised, and, as it dropped, he dropped with it, and I laid him down dead. * * * *

'When I returned to the bedside of the young woman, I found her raving in precisely the same order and continuity. I knew that this might last for many hours, and that it would probably end in the silence of the grave.

'I repeated the medicines I had given her, and I sat at the side of the bed until the night was far advanced.

' "Is she dead?" asked the Marquis, whom I will still describe as the elder brother, coming into the room.

' "Not dead," said I; "but like to die."

' "What strength there is in these common bodies!" he said, looking down at her with some curiosity.

' "There is prodigious strength," I answered him, "in sorrow and despair."

'He first laughed at my words, and then frowned at them. He moved a chair with his foot near to mine, and said in a subdued voice:

' "Doctor, finding my brother in this difficulty with these hinds, I recommended that your aid should be invited. Your reputation is high, and, as a young man with your fortune to make, you are probably mindful of your interest. The things that you see here, are things to be seen, and not spoken of."

'I listened to the patient's breathing, and avoided answering.

' "Do you honour me with your attention, Doctor?"

' "Monsieur," said I, "in my profession, the communications of patients are always received in confidence." I was guarded in my answer, for I was troubled in my mind with what I had heard and seen.

'Her breathing was so difficult to trace, that I carefully tried the pulse and the heart. There was life, and no more. Looking round as I resumed my seat, I found both the brothers intent upon me. * * * *

'I write with so much difficulty, the cold is so severe, I am so fearful of being detected and consigned to an underground cell and total darkness, that I must abridge this narrative. There is no confusion or failure in my memory; it can recall, and could detail, every word that was ever spoken between me and those brothers.

'She lingered for a week. Towards the last, I could understand some few syllables that she said to me by placing my ear close to her lips. She asked me where she was, and I told her; who I was, and I told her. It was in vain that I asked her for her family name. She faintly shook her head upon the pillow, and kept her secret, as the boy had done.

'As often as I caught the younger brother's eyes, their expression reminded me that he disliked me deeply, for knowing what I knew from the boy. I also saw that I was an incumbrance in the mind of the elder, too.

'My patient died, two hours before midnight. I was alone with her, when her forlorn young head dropped gently on one side, and all her earthly wrongs and sorrows ended.

'The brothers were waiting in a room down-stairs, impatient to ride away. I had heard them, alone at the bedside, striking their boots with their riding-whips, and loitering up and down.

' "At last she is dead?" said the elder, when I went in.

' "She is dead," said I.

' "I congratulate you, my brother," were his words as he turned round.

'He had before offered me money, which I had postponed taking. He now gave me a rouleau of gold. I took it from his hand, but laid it on the table. I had considered the question, and had resolved to accept nothing.

' "Pray excuse me," said I. "Under the circumstances, no."

'They exchanged looks, but bent their heads to me as I bent mine to them, and we parted without another word on either side. * * * *

'I am weary, weary, weary—worn down by misery. I cannot read what I have written with this gaunt hand.

'Early in the morning, the rouleau of gold was left at my door in a little box, with my name on the outside. From the first, I had anxiously considered what I ought to do. I decided, that day, to write privately to the Minister, stating all the circumstances. I knew what Court influence was, and what the immunities of the Nobles were, and I expected that the matter would never be heard of; but, I wished to relieve my own mind. I had kept the matter a profound secret, even from my wife; and this, too, I resolved to state in my letter.

'I was much engaged that day, and could not complete my letter that night. I rose long before my usual time next morning to finish it. It was the last day of the year. The letter was lying before me just completed, when I was told that a lady waited, who wished to see me. * * * *

'I am growing more and more unequal to the task I have set myself. It is so cold, so dark, my senses are so benumbed, and the gloom upon me is so dreadful.

'The lady was young, engaging, and handsome, but not marked for long life. She was in great agitation. She presented herself to me as the wife of the Marquis St. Evrémonde. I connected the title by which the boy had addressed the elder brother, with the initial letter embroidered on the scarf, and had no difficulty in arriving at the conclusion that I had seen that nobleman very lately.

'My memory is still accurate, but I cannot write the words of our conversation. I suspect that I am watched more closely than I was, and I know not at what time I may be watched. She had discovered the main facts of the cruel story, of her husband's share in it, and my being resorted to. She did not know that the girl was dead. Her hope had been, she said in great distress, to show her, in secret, a woman's sympathy.

'She had reasons for believing that there was a young sister living, and her greatest desire was, to help that sister. I could tell her nothing but that there was such a sister; beyond that, I knew nothing. Her inducement to come to me had been the hope that I could tell her the name and place of abode. Whereas, to this wretched hour I am ignorant of both. * * * *

'These scraps of paper fail me. One was taken from me, with a warning, yesterday. I must finish my record to-day.

'She was a good, compassionate lady, and not happy in her marriage. How could she be! The brother distrusted and disliked her, and his influence was all opposed to her; she stood in dread of him, and in dread of her husband too. When I took her down to the door, there was a child, a pretty boy from two to three years old, in her carriage.

' "For his sake, Doctor," she said, pointing to him in tears, "I would do all I can to make what poor amends I can. He will never prosper in his inheritance otherwise. I have a presentiment that if no other innocent atonement is made for this, it will one day be required of him. What I have left to call my own—it is little beyond the worth of a few jewels—I will make it the first charge of his life to bestow on this injured family, if the sister can be discovered."

'She kissed the boy, and said, caressing him, "It is for thine own dear sake. Thou wilt be faithful, little Charles?" The child answered her bravely, "Yes!" I kissed her hand, and she took him in her arms, and went away caressing him. I never saw her more.

'As she had mentioned her husband's name in the faith that I knew it, I added no mention of it to my letter. I sealed my letter, and, not trusting it out of my own hands, delivered it myself that day.

'That night, the last night of the year, towards nine o'clock, a man in a black dress rang at my gate, demanded to see me, and softly followed my servant, Ernest Defarge, a youth, upstairs. When my servant came into the room where I sat with my wife—O my wife, beloved of my heart!—we saw the man, who was supposed to be at the gate, standing silent behind him.

'An urgent case in the Rue St. Honoré, he said. It would not detain me, he had a coach in waiting.

'It brought me here, it brought me to my grave. When I was clear of the house, a black muffler was drawn tightly over my mouth from behind, and my arms were pinioned. The two brothers crossed the road from a dark corner, and identified me with a single gesture. The Marquis took from his pocket the letter I had written, showed it me, burnt it in the light of a lantern that was held, and extinguished the ashes with his foot. Not a word was spoken. I was brought here, I was brought to my living grave.

'If it had pleased GOD to put it in the hard heart of either of the brothers, in all these frightful years, to grant me any tidings of my dearest wife—so much as to let me know by a word whether alive or dead—I might have thought that He had not quite abandoned them. But, now I believe that the mark of the red cross is fatal to them, and that they have no part in His mercies. And them and their descendants, to the last of their race, I, Alexandre Manette, unhappy prisoner, do this last night of the year 1767, in my unbearable agony, denounce to the times when all these things shall be answered for. I denounce them to Heaven and to earth.'

A terrible sound arose when the reading of this document was done. A sound of craving and eagerness that had nothing articulate in it but blood. The narrative called up the most revengeful passions of the time, and there was not a head in the nation but must have dropped before it.

Little need, in presence of that tribunal, to show how the Defarges had not made the paper public, with the other captured Bastille memorials borne in procession, and had kept it, biding their time. Little need to show that this detested family name had long been anathematized by Saint Antoine, and was wrought into the fatal register. The man never trod ground whose virtues and services would have sustained him in that place that day, against such denunciation.

'Much influence around him, has that Doctor?' murmured Madame Defarge, smiling to The Vengeance. 'Save him now, my Doctor, save him!'

At every juryman's vote, there was a roar. Another and another. Roar and roar.

Unanimously voted. At heart and by descent an Aristocrat, an enemy of the Republic, a notorious oppressor of the People. Back to the Conciergerie, and Death within four-and-twenty hours!

The wretched wife of the innocent man thus doomed to die, fell under the sentence, as if she had been mortally stricken. But, she uttered no sound; and so strong was the voice within her, representing that it was she of all the world who must uphold him in his misery and not augment it, that it quickly raised her, even from that shock.

The judges having to take part in a public demonstration out of doors, the tribunal adjourned. The quick noise and movement of the court's emptying itself by many passages had not ceased, when Lucie stood stretching out her arms towards her husband, with nothing in her face but love and consolation.

'If I might touch him! If I might embrace him once! O, good citizens, if you would have so much compassion for us!'

There was but a gaoler left, along with two of the four men who had taken him last night. One said, 'Let her embrace him then; it is but a moment.' It was silently acquiesced in, and they passed her to a raised place, where he, by leaning over the dock, could fold her in his arms.

'Farewell, dear darling of my soul. My parting blessing on my love. We shall meet again, where the weary are at rest!'

They were her husband's words, as he held her to his bosom.

'I can bear it, dear Charles. I am supported from above: don't suffer for me. A parting blessing for our child.'

'I send it to her by you. I kiss her by you. I say farewell to her by you.'

Her father had followed her, and would have fallen on his knees to both of them, but that Darnay put out a hand and seized him, crying:

'No, no! What have you done, what have you done, that you should kneel to us! We know now, what a struggle you made of old. We know now, what you underwent when you suspected my descent, and when you knew it. We know now, what you strove against, and conquered, for her dear sake. We thank you with all our hearts. Heaven be with you!'

Her father's only answer was to draw his hands through his white hair, and wring them with a shriek of anguish.

'It could not be otherwise,' said the prisoner. 'All things have worked together as they have fallen out. It was the always-vain endeavour to discharge my poor mother's trust that first brought my fatal presence near you. Good could never come of such evil, a happier end was not in nature to so unhappy a beginning. Be comforted, and forgive me. Heaven bless you!'

As he was drawn away, his wife released him, and stood looking after him with her hands touching one another in the attitude of prayer, and with a radiant look upon her face, in which there was even a comforting smile. As he went out at the prisoners' door, she turned, laid her head lovingly on her father's breast, tried to speak to him, and fell at his feet.

Then, issuing from the obscure corner from which he had never moved, Sydney Carton came and took her up. Only her father and Mr. Lorry were with her. His arm trembled as it raised her, and supported her head. Yet, there was an air about him that was not all of pity—that had a flush of pride in it.

'Shall I take her to a coach? I shall never feel her weight.'

He carried her lightly to the door, and laid her tenderly down in a coach. Her father and their old friend got into it, and he took his seat beside the driver.

When they arrived at the gateway where he had paused in the dark not many hours before, to picture to himself on which of the rough stones of the street her feet had trodden, he lifted her again, and carried her up the staircase to their rooms. There, he laid her down on a couch, where her child and Miss Pross wept over her.

'Don't recall her to herself,' he said, softly, to the latter, 'she is better so. Don't revive her to consciousness, while she only faints.'

'Oh, Carton, Carton, dear Carton!' cried little Lucie, springing up and throwing her arms passionately round him, in a burst of grief. 'Now that you have come, I think you will do something to help mamma, something to save papa!

O, look at her, dear Carton! Can you, of all the people who love her, bear to see her so?'

He bent over the child, and laid her blooming cheek against his face. He put her gently from him, and looked at her unconscious mother.

'Before I go,' he said, and paused—'I may kiss her?'

It was remembered afterwards that when he bent down and touched her face with his lips, he murmured some words. The child, who was nearest to him, told them afterwards, that she heard him say, 'A life you love.'

When he had gone out into the next room, he turned suddenly on Mr. Lorry and her father, who were following, and said to the latter:

'You had great influence but yesterday, Doctor Manette; let it at least be tried. These judges, and all the men in power, are very friendly to you, and very recognisant of your services; are they not?'

'Nothing connected with Charles was concealed from me. I had the strongest assurances that I should save him; and I did.' He returned the answer in great trouble, and very slowly.

'Try them again. The hours between this and to-morrow afternoon are few and short, but try.'

'I intend to try. I will not rest a moment.'

'That's well. I have known such energy as yours do great things before now—though never,' he added, with a smile and a sigh together, 'such great things as this. But try!'

'I will go,' said Doctor Manette, 'to the Prosecutor and the President straight, and I will go to others whom it is better not to name. I will write too, and—— But stay! There is a celebration in the streets, and no one will be accessible until dark.'

'That's true. Well! It is a forlorn hope at the best, and not much the forlorner for being delayed till dark. If I go to Mr. Lorry's at nine, shall I hear what you have done, either from our friend or from yourself?'

'Yes.'

'May you prosper!'

Mr. Lorry followed Sydney to the outer door, and, touching him on the shoulder as he was going away, caused him to turn.

'I have no hope,' said Mr. Lorry, in a low and sorrowful whisper.

'Nor have I.'

'If any one of these men, or all of these men, were disposed to spare him—which is a large supposition; for what is his life, or any man's to them!—I doubt if they durst spare him after the demonstration in the court.'

'And so do I. I heard the fall of the axe in that sound.'

Mr. Lorry leaned his arm upon the door-post, and bowed his face upon it.

'Don't despond,' said Carton, very gently; 'don't grieve. I encouraged Doctor Manette in this idea, because I felt that it might one day be consolatory to her.'

'Yes, yes, yes,' returned Mr. Lorry, drying his eyes, 'you are right. But he will perish; there is no real hope.'

'Yes. He will perish: there is no real hope,' echoed Carton. And walked with a settled step, downstairs.

---

19 · DARKNESS

SYDNEY CARTON paused in the street, not quite decided where to go. 'At Tellson's banking-house at nine,' he said, with a musing face. 'Shall I do well, in the mean time, to show myself? I think so. It is best that these people should know there is such a man as I here; it is a sound precaution, and may be a necessary preparation. It is best,' he said, finally resolved, 'that these people should know there is such a man as I here.' And he turned his face towards Saint Antoine.

Defarge had described himself, that day, as the keeper of a wine-shop in the Saint Antoine suburb. It was not difficult for one who knew the city well, to find his house without asking any question. Having ascertained its situation, Carton came out of those closer streets again, and dined at a place of refreshment and fell sound asleep after dinner. For the first time in many years, he had no strong drink. Since last night he had taken nothing but a little light thin wine, and last night he had dropped the brandy slowly down on Mr. Lorry's hearth like a man who had done with it.

It was as late as seven o'clock when he awoke refreshed, and went out into the streets again. As he passed along towards Saint Antoine, he stopped at a shop-window where there was a mirror, and slightly altered the disordered arrangement of his loose cravat, and his coat-collar, and his wild hair. This done, he went on direct to Defarge's, and went in.

There happened to be no customer in the shop but Jacques Three. This man stood drinking at the little counter, in conversation with the Defarges, man and wife. The Vengeance assisted in the conversation, like a regular member of the establishment.

As Carton walked in, took his seat and asked (in very poor French) for a small measure of wine, Madame Defarge cast a careless glance at him, and then a keener, and then a keener, and then advanced to him herself, and asked him what it was he had ordered.

He repeated what he had already said.

'English?' asked Madame Defarge, inquisitively raising her dark eyebrows.

After looking at her, as if the sound of even a single French word were slow to express itself to him, he answered, in his former strong foreign accent, 'Yes, madame, yes. I am English!'

Madame Defarge returned to her counter to get the wine, and, as he took up a Jacobin journal and feigned to puzzle out its meaning, he heard her say, 'I swear to you, like Evrémonde!'

Defarge brought him the wine, and gave him Good Evening.

'How?'

'Good evening.'

'Oh! Good evening, citizen,' filling his glass. 'Ah! and good wine. I drink to the Republic.'

Defarge went back to the counter, and said, 'Certainly, a little like.' Madame sternly retorted, 'I tell you a good deal like.' Jacques Three pacifically remarked, 'He is so much in your mind, see you, madame.' The amiable Vengeance added, with a laugh, 'Yes, my faith! And you are looking forward with so much pleasure to seeing him once more to-morrow!'

Carton followed the lines and words of his paper, with a slow forefinger. They were all leaning their arms on the counter close together, speaking low. After a silence of a few moments, during which they all looked towards him without disturbing his outward attention from the Jacobin editor, they resumed their conversation.

'It is true what madame says,' observed Jacques Three. 'Why stop? There is great force in that. Why stop?'

'Well, well,' reasoned Defarge, 'but one must stop somewhere. After all, the question is still where?'

'At extermination,' said madame.

'Magnificent!' croaked Jacques Three. The Vengeance, also, highly approved.

'Extermination is good doctrine, my wife,' said Defarge, rather troubled; 'in general, I say nothing against it. But this Doctor has suffered much; you have seen him to-day; you have observed his face when the paper was read.'

'I have observed his face!' repeated madame, contemptuously and angrily. 'Yes. I have observed his face. I have observed his face to be not the face of a true friend of the Republic. Let him take care of his face!'

'And you have observed, my wife,' said Defarge, in a deprecatory manner, 'the anguish of his daughter, which must be a dreadful anguish to him!'

'I have observed his daughter,' repeated madame; 'yes, I have observed his daughter, more times than one. I have observed her to-day, and I have observed her other days. I have observed her in the court, and I have observed her in the street by the prison. Let me but lift my finger——!' She seemed to raise it (the listener's eyes were always on his paper), and to let it fall with a rattle on the ledge before her, as if the axe had dropped.

'As to thee,' pursued madame, implacably, addressing her husband, 'if it depended on thee—which, happily, it does not—thou wouldst rescue this man even now.'

'No!' protested Defarge. 'Not if to lift this glass would do it! But I would leave the matter there. I say, stop there.'

'See you then, Jacques,' said Madame Defarge, wrathfully; 'and see you, too, my little Vengeance; see you both! Listen! For other crimes as tyrants and oppressors, I have this race a long time on my register, doomed to destruction and extermination. Ask my husband, is that so.'

'It is so,' assented Defarge, without being asked.

'In the beginning of the great days, when the Bastille falls, he finds this paper of to-day, and he brings it home, and in the middle of the night when this place is clear and shut, we read it, here on this spot, by the light of this lamp. Ask him, is that so.'

'It is so,' assented Defarge.

'That night, I tell him, that I have now a secret to communicate. Ask him, is that so.'

'It is so,' assented Defarge again.

'I tell him, "Defarge, I was brought up among the fishermen of the sea-shore, and that peasant family so injured by the two Evrémonde brothers, as that Bastille paper describes, is my family. Defarge, that sister of the mortally wounded boy upon the ground was my sister, that husband was my sister's husband, that brother was my brother, that father was my father, those dead are my dead, and that summons to answer for those things descends to me!" Ask him, is that so.'

'It is so,' assented Defarge once more.

'Then tell Wind and Fire where to stop,' returned madame; 'but don't tell me.'

Customers entered, and the group was broken up. The English customer paid for what he had had, perplexedly counted his change, and asked, as a stranger, to be directed towards the National Palace.

He went his way, and was soon swallowed up in the shadow of the night. At the appointed hour he presented himself in Mr. Lorry's room again, where he found the old gentleman walking to and fro in restless anxiety. He said he had been with Lucie until just now, and had only left her for a few minutes, to come and keep his appointment. Her father had not been seen, since he quitted the banking-house towards four o'clock.

Mr. Lorry waited until ten; but, Doctor Manette not returning, and he being unwilling to leave Lucie any longer, it was arranged that he should go back to her, and come to the banking-house again at midnight. In the meanwhile, Carton would wait alone by the fire for the Doctor.

He waited and waited, and the clock struck twelve; but Doctor Manette did not come back. Mr. Lorry returned, and found no tidings of him, and brought none. Where could he be?

They were discussing this question, and were almost building up some weak structure of hope on his prolonged absence, when they heard him on the stairs. The instant he entered the room, it was plain that all was lost.

As he stood staring at them, they asked him no question, for his face told them everything.

'I cannot find it,' said he, 'and I must have it. Where is it?'

His head and throat were bare, and, as he spoke with a helpless look straying all around, he took his coat off, and let it drop on the floor.

'Where is my bench? I have been looking everywhere for my bench, and I can't find it. What have they done with my work? Time presses: I must finish those shoes.'

Lost, utterly lost!

It was so clearly beyond hope to reason with him, or try to restore him,—that—as if by agreement—they each put a hand upon his shoulder, and soothed him to sit down before the fire, with a promise that he should have his work presently. He sank into the chair, and brooded over the embers, and shed tears. As if all that had happened since the garret time were a momentary fancy, or a dream, Mr. Lorry saw him shrink into the exact figure that Defarge had had in keeping. Carton was the first to speak:

'The last chance is gone: it was not much. He had better be taken to her. But, before you go, will you, for a moment, steadily attend to me? Don't ask me why I make the stipulations I am going to make, and exact the promise I am going to exact; I have a reason—a good one.'

'I do not doubt it,' answered Mr. Lorry. 'Say on.'

The figure in the chair between them, was all the time monotonously rocking itself to and fro, and moaning. They spoke in such a tone as they would have used if they had been watching by a sick-bed in the night.

Carton stooped to pick up the coat, which lay almost entangling his feet. As he did so, a small case in which the Doctor was accustomed to carry the list of his day's duties, fell lightly on the floor. Carton took it up, and there was a folded paper in it. 'We should look at this!' he said. Mr. Lorry nodded his consent. He opened it, and exclaimed, 'Thank GOD!'

'What is it?' asked Mr. Lorry, eagerly.

'A moment! Let me speak of it in its place. First,' he put his hand in his coat, and took another paper from it, 'that is the certificate which enables me to pass out of this city. Look at it. You see—Sydney Carton, an Englishman?'

Mr. Lorry held it open in his hand, gazing in his earnest face.

'Keep it for me until to-morrow. I shall see him to-morrow, you remember, and I had better not take it into the prison.'

'Why not?'

'I don't know; I prefer not to do so. Now, take this paper that Doctor Manette has carried about him. It is a similar certificate, enabling him and his daughter and her child, at any time, to pass the Barrier and the frontier? You see?'

'Yes!'

'Put it up carefully with mine and your own. Now, listen! It is good, until recalled. But it may be soon recalled, and, I have reason to think, will be.'

'They are not in danger?'

'They are in great danger. They are in danger of denunciation by Madame Defarge. I know it from her own lips. I have overheard words of that woman's, to-night, which have presented their danger to me in strong colours. I have lost no time, and since then, I have seen the spy. He confirms me. He knows that a wood-sawyer, living by the prison-wall, is under the control of the Defarges, and has been rehearsed by Madame Defarge as to his having seen Her'—he never mentioned Lucie's name—'making signs and signals to prisoners. It is easy to foresee that the pretence will be the common one, a prison plot, and that it will involve her life—and perhaps her child's—and perhaps her father's—for both have been seen with her at that place. Don't look so horrified. You will save them all.'

'Heaven grant I may, Carton! But how?'

'I am going to tell you how. It will depend on you, and it could depend on no better man. This new denunciation will certainly not take place until after to-morrow. You have money, and can buy the means of travelling to the sea-coast as quickly as the journey can be made. Your preparations have been completed for some days, to return to England.

Early to-morrow have your horses ready, so that they may be in starting trim at two o'clock in the afternoon.'

'It shall be done!'

His manner was so fervent and inspiring, that Mr. Lorry caught the flame, and was as quick as youth.

'You are a noble heart. Did I say we could depend upon no better man? Tell her, to-night, what you know of her danger as involving her child and her father. Dwell upon that, for she would lay her own fair head beside her husband's cheerfully.' He faltered for an instant; then went on as before. 'For the sake of her child and her father, press upon her the necessity of leaving Paris, with them and you, at that hour. Tell her that it was her husband's last arrangement. Tell her that more depends upon it than she dare believe, or hope. You think that her father, even in this sad state, will submit himself to her; do you not?'

'I am sure of it.'

'I thought so. Quietly and steadily have all these arrangements made in the court-yard here, even to the taking of your own seat in the carriage. The moment I come to you, take me in, and drive away.'

'I understand that I wait for you under all circumstances?'

'You have my certificate in your hand with the rest, you know, and will reserve my place. Wait for nothing but to have my place occupied, and then for England!'

'Why, then,' said Mr. Lorry, grasping his eager but so firm and steady hand, 'it does not all depend on one old man, but I shall have a young and ardent man at my side.'

'By the help of Heaven you shall! Promise me solemnly that nothing will influence you to alter the course on which we now stand pledged to one another.'

'Nothing, Carton.'

'Remember these words to-morrow: change the course, or delay in it—for any reason—and no life can possibly be saved, and many lives must inevitably be sacrificed.'

'I will remember them. I hope to do my part faithfully.'

'And I hope to do mine. Now, good-bye!'

Though he said it with a grave smile of earnestness, and though he even put the old man's hand to his lips, he did not part from him then. He helped him so far as to arouse the rocking figure before the dying embers, as to get a cloak and hat put upon it, and to tempt it forth to find where the bench and work were hidden. He walked on the other side of it and protected it to the court-yard of the house. He entered the court-yard and remained there for a few moments alone, looking up at the light in the window of her room. Before he went away, he breathed a blessing towards it, and a Farewell.

---

20 · FIFTY-TWO

In the black prison of the Conciergerie, the doomed of the day awaited their fate. They were in number as the weeks of the year. Fifty-two were to roll that afternoon on the life-tide of the city to the boundless everlasting sea.

Charles Darnay, alone in a cell, had sustained himself with no flattering delusion since he came to it from the Tribunal. In every line of the narrative he had heard, he had heard his condemnation.

Nevertheless, it was not easy, with the face of his beloved wife fresh before him, to compose his mind to what it must bear. But by degrees he calmed into the better state, when he could raise his thoughts much higher, and draw comfort down. Before it had set in dark on the night of his condemnation, he had travelled thus far on his last way. When he lay down on his straw bed, he thought he had done with this world.

He had been apprised that the final hour was Three, and he knew he would be summoned some time earlier, inasmuch as the tumbrils jolted heavily and slowly through the streets. Therefore, he resolved to keep Two before his mind, as the hour, and so to strengthen himself in the interval that he might be able, after that time, to strengthen others.

Walking regularly to and fro with his arms folded, he heard One struck away from him, without surprise.

Footsteps in the stone passage outside the door.

The key was put in the lock, and turned. Before the door was opened, or as it opened, a man said in a low voice, in English: 'He has never seen me here; I have kept out of his way. Go you in alone; I wait near. Lose no time!'

The door was quickly opened and closed, and there stood before him face to face, quiet, intent upon him, with the light of a smile on his features, and a cautionary finger on his lip, Sydney Carton.

'Of all the people upon earth, you least expected to see me?' he said.

'I could not believe it to be you. I can scarcely believe it now. You are not'—the apprehension came suddenly into his mind—'a prisoner?'

'No. I am accidentally possessed of a power over one of the keepers here, and in virtue of it I stand before you. I come from her—your wife, dear Darnay.'

The prisoner wrung his hand.

'I bring you a request from her.'

'What is it?'

'You have no time to ask me why I bring it, or what it means; I have no time to tell you. You must comply with it—take off those boots you wear, and draw on these of mine.'

There was a chair against the wall of the cell, behind the prisoner. Carton, pressing forward, had already, with the speed of lightning, got him down into it, and stood over him, barefoot.

'Draw on these boots of mine. Quick!'

'Carton, there is no escaping from this place; it never can be done. You will only die with me. It is madness.'

'It would be madness if I asked you to escape; but do I? When I ask you to pass out at that door, tell me it is madness and remain here. Change that cravat for this of mine, that coat for this of mine. While you do it, let me take this ribbon from your hair, and shake out your hair like this of mine!'

With wonderful quickness, and with a strength both of will and action, he forced all these changes upon him.

'Carton! Dear Carton! It is madness. It cannot be accomplished, it never can be done, it has been attempted, and has always failed. I implore you not to add your death to the bitterness of mine.'

'Do I ask you, my dear Darnay, to pass the door? When I ask that, refuse. There are pen and ink and paper on this table. Is your hand steady enough to write?'

'It was when you came in.'

'Steady it again, and write what I shall dictate. Quick, friend, quick!'

Pressing his hand to his bewildered head, Darnay sat down at the table. Carton, with his right hand in his breast, stood close beside him.

'Write exactly as I speak.'

'To whom do I address it?'

'To no one.' Carton still had his hand in his breast.

'Do I date it?'

'No.'

The prisoner looked up, at each question. Carton, standing over him with his hand in his breast, looked down.

' "If you remember," ' said Carton, dictating, ' "the words that passed between us, long ago, you will readily comprehend this when you see it. You do remember them, I know. It is not in your nature to forget them." '

He was drawing his hand from his breast; the prisoner chancing to look up in his hurried wonder as he wrote, the hand stopped, closing upon something.

'Have you written "forget them"?' Carton asked.

'I have. Is that a weapon in your hand?'

'No; I am not armed.'

'What is it in your hand?'

'You shall know directly. Write on; there are but a few words more.' He dictated again. ' "I am thankful that the time has come when I can prove them. That I do so is no subject for regret or grief." ' As he said these words with his eyes fixed on the writer, his hand slowly and softly moved down close to the writer's face.

The pen dropped from Darnay's fingers on the table, and he looked about him vacantly.

'What vapour is that?' he asked.

'Vapour?'

'Something that crossed me?'

'I am conscious of nothing; there can be nothing here. Take up the pen and finish. Hurry, hurry!'

As if his memory were impaired, or his faculties disordered, the prisoner made an effort to rally his attention. As he looked at Carton with clouded eyes and with an altered manner of breathing, Carton—his hand again in his breast—looked steadily at him.

'Hurry, hurry!'

The prisoner bent over the paper, once more.

' "If it had been otherwise;" ' Carton's hand was again watchfully and softly stealing down; ' "I never should have used the longer opportunity. If it had been otherwise;" ' the hand was at the prisoner's face: ' "I should but have had so much the more to answer for. If it had been otherwise——" ' Carton looked at the pen and saw it was trailing off into unintelligible signs.

Carton's hand moved back to his breast no more. The prisoner sprang up with a reproachful look, but Carton's hand was close and firm at his nostrils, and Carton's left arm caught him round the waist. For a few seconds he faintly struggled with the man who had come to lay down his life for him; but, within a minute or so, he was stretched insensible on the ground.

Quickly, but with hands as true to the purpose as his heart was, Carton dressed himself in the clothes the prisoner had laid aside, combed back his hair, and tied it with the ribbon the prisoner had worn. Then, he softly called, 'Enter there! Come in!' and the Spy presented himself.

'You see?' said Carton, looking up, as he kneeled on one knee beside the insensible figure, putting the paper in the breast: 'is your hazard very great?'

'Mr. Carton,' the Spy answered, with a timid snap of his fingers, 'my hazard is not *that*, in the thick of business here, if you are true to the whole of your bargain.'

'Don't fear me. I will be true to the death.'

'You must be, Mr. Carton, if the tale of fifty-two is to be

right. Being made right by you in that dress, I shall have no fear.'

'Have no fear! I shall soon be out of the way of harming you, and the rest will soon be far from here, please God! Now, get assistance and take me to the coach.'

'You?' said the Spy nervously.

'Him, man, with whom I have exchanged. You go out at the gate by which you brought me in?'

'Of course.'

'I was weak and faint when you brought me in, and I am fainter now you take me out. The parting interview has overpowered me. Such a thing has happened here, often, and too often. Quick! Call assistance!'

'You swear not to betray me?' said the trembling Spy, as he paused for a last moment.

'Man, man!' returned Carton, stamping his foot; 'have I sworn by no solemn vow already, to go through with this, that you waste the precious moments now? Take him yourself to the court-yard you know of, place him yourself in the carriage, show him yourself to Mr. Lorry, tell him yourself to give him no restorative but air, and to remember my words of last night, and his promise of last night, and drive away!'

The Spy withdrew, and Carton seated himself at the table, resting his forehead on his hands. The Spy returned immediately, with two men.

'How, then?' said one of them, contemplating the fallen figure. 'So afflicted to find that his friend has drawn a prize in the lottery of Sainte Guillotine?'

'A good patriot,' said the other, 'could hardly have been more afflicted if the Aristocrat had drawn a blank.'

They raised the unconscious figure, placed it on a litter they had brought to the door, and bent to carry it away.

'The time is short, Evrémonde,' said the Spy, in a warning voice.

'I know it well,' answered Carton. 'Be careful of my friend, I entreat you, and leave me.'

'Come, then, my children,' said Barsad. 'Lift him, and come away!'

The door closed, and Carton was left alone. Straining his powers of listening to the utmost, he listened for any sound that might denote suspicion or alarm. There was none. Keys turned, doors clashed, footsteps passed along distant passages: no cry was raised, or hurry made, that seemed unusual. Breathing more freely in a little while, he sat down at the table, and listened again until the clock struck Two.

Sounds that he was not afraid of, for he divined the meaning, then began to be audible. Several doors were opened in succession, and finally his own. A gaoler, with a list in his hand, looked in, merely saying, 'Follow me, Evrémonde!' and he followed into a large dark room, at a distance. It was a dark winter day, and he could but dimly discern the others who were brought there to have their arms bound.

As he stood by the wall in a dim corner, a young woman, with a slight girlish form, a sweet spare face in which there was no vestige of colour, and large widely opened patient eyes, rose from the seat where he had observed her sitting, and came to speak to him.

'Citizen Evrémonde,' she said, touching him with her cold hand. 'I am a poor little seamstress, who was with you in La Force.'

He murmured for answer: 'True. I forget what you were accused of?'

'Plots. Though the just Heaven knows I am innocent of

any. Is it likely? Who would think of plotting with a poor little weak creature like me?'

The forlorn smile with which she said it, so touched him, that tears started from his eyes.

'I am not afraid to die, Citizen Evrémonde, but I have done nothing. I am not unwilling to die, if the Republic which is to do so much good to us poor, will profit by my death; but I do not know how that can be, Citizen Evrémonde. Such a poor weak little creature!'

As the last thing on earth that his heart was to warm and soften to, it warmed and softened to this pitiable girl.

'I heard you were released, Citizen Evrémonde. I hoped it was true?'

'It was. But, I was again taken and condemned.'

'If I may ride with you, Citizen Evrémonde, will you let me hold your hand? I am not afraid, but I am little and weak, and it will give me more courage.'

As the patient eyes were lifted to his face, he saw a sudden doubt in them, and then astonishment. He pressed the work-worn, hunger-worn young fingers, and touched his lips.

'Are you dying for him?' she whispered.

'And his wife and child. Hush! Yes.'

'O you will let me hold your brave hand, stranger?'

'Hush! Yes, my poor sister; to the last.'

The same shadows that are falling on the prison, are falling, in that same hour of the early afternoon, on the Barrier with the crowd about it, when a coach going out of Paris drives up to be examined.

'Who goes here? Whom have we within? Papers!'

The papers are handed out, and read.

'Alexandre Manette. Physician. French. Which is he?'

This is he; this helpless, wandering old man pointed out.

'Apparently the Citizen-Doctor is not in his right mind? The Revolution-fever will have been too much for him?'

Greatly too much for him.

'Hah! Many suffer with it. Lucie. His daughter. French. Which is she?'

This is she.

'Apparently it must be. Lucie, the wife of Evrémonde; is it not?'

It is.

'Hah! Evrémonde has an assignation elsewhere. Lucie, her child. English. This is she?'

She and no other.

'Kiss me, child of Evrémonde. Now, thou hast kissed a good Republican; something new in thy family; remember it! Sydney Carton. Advocate. English. Which is he?'

He lies here, in this corner of the carriage. He, too, is pointed out.

'Apparently the English advocate is in a swoon?'

It is hoped he will recover in the fresher air. It is represented that he is not in strong health, and has separated sadly from a friend who is under the displeasure of the Republic.

'Is that all? It is not a great deal, that! Many are under the displeasure of the Republic, and must look out at the little window. Jarvis Lorry. Banker. English. Which is he?'

'I am he. Necessarily, being the last.'

It is Jarvis Lorry who has replied to all the previous questions. It is Jarvis Lorry who has alighted and stands with his hand on the coach door, replying to a group of officials. They leisurely walk round the carriage and leisurely mount the box, to look at what little luggage it carries on the roof; the country-people hanging about, press nearer to the coach doors and greedily stare in.

'Behold your papers, Jarvis Lorry, countersigned.'

'One can depart, citizen?'

'One can depart. A good journey!'

'I salute you, citizens.—And the first danger passed!'

These are again the words of Jarvis Lorry, as he clasps his hands, and looks upward. There is terror in the carriage, there is weeping, there is the heavy breathing of the insensible traveller.

'Are we not going too slowly? Can they not be induced to go faster?' asks Lucie, clinging to the old man.

'It would seem like flight, my darling. I must not urge them too much: it would rouse suspicion.'

'Look back, look back, and see if we are pursued!'

'The road is clear, my dearest. So far, we are not pursued.'

At the same time as the Fifty-Two awaited their fate, Madame Defarge held dark council with The Vengeance and Jacques Three in the shed of the wood-sawyer, the former mender of roads.

'But our Defarge,' said Jacques Three, 'is undoubtedly a good Republican? Eh?'

'There is no better,' the voluble Vengeance protested in her shrill notes, 'in France.'

'Peace, little Vengeance,' said Madame Defarge, laying her hand with a slight frown on her lieutenant's lips, 'hear me speak. My husband, fellow-citizens, is a good Republican and a bold man; he has deserved well of the Republic, and possesses its confidence. But my husband has his weaknesses, and he is so weak as to relent towards this Doctor.'

'It is a great pity,' croaked Jacques Three, dubiously

shaking his head; 'it is not quite like a good citizen; it is a thing to regret.'

'See you,' said madame, 'I care nothing for this Doctor, I. He may wear his head or lose it; it is all one to me. But, the Evrémonde people are to be exterminated, and the wife and child must follow the husband and father.'

Madame Defarge reflected, then said:

'I cannot trust my husband in this matter. Not only do I feel, since last night, that I dare not confide to him the details of my projects; but also I feel that if I delay, there is danger of his giving warning, and then they might escape. I must act for myself, therefore. Come hither, little citizen.'

The wood-sawyer, who held her in the respect, and himself in the submission, of mortal fear, advanced with his hand to his red cap.

'Touching those signals, little citizen,' said Madame Defarge, sternly, 'that she made to the prisoners; you are ready to bear witness to them this very day?'

'Ay, ay, why not!' cried the sawyer. 'Every day, in all weathers, from two to four, always signalling, sometimes with the little one, sometimes without. I know what I know. I have seen with my eyes.'

Madame Defarge beckoned the Juryman and The Vengeance a little nearer to the door, and there expounded her further views to them thus:

'She will now be at home, awaiting the moment of his death. She will be mourning and grieving. She will be in a state of mind to impeach the justice of the Republic. I will go to her.'

'What an admirable woman; what an adorable woman!' exclaimed Jacques Three, rapturously. 'Ah, my cherished!' cried The Vengeance; and embraced her.

'Take you my knitting,' said Madame Defarge, placing it in her lieutenant's hands, 'and have it ready for me in my usual seat. Keep me my usual chair. Go you there, straight, for there will probably be a greater concourse than usual, to-day.'

'I willingly obey the orders of my Chief,' said The Vengeance with alacrity, kissing her cheek. 'You will not be late?'

'I shall be there before the commencement.'

'And before the tumbrils arrive. Be sure you are there, my soul,' said The Vengeance, calling after her, for she had already turned into the street, 'before the tumbrils arrive!'

Madame Defarge slightly waved her hand, to imply that she heard, and might be relied upon to arrive in good time, and so went through the mud, and round the corner of the prison wall. There were many women at that time, upon whom the time laid a dreadfully disfiguring hand; but, there was not one among them more to be dreaded than this ruthless woman, now taking her way along the streets. Lying hidden in her bosom, was a loaded pistol. Lying hidden at her waist, was a sharpened dagger. Thus accoutred, Madame Defarge took her way along the streets.

Now, when the journey of the travelling coach, at that very moment waiting for the completion of its load, had been planned out last night, the difficulty of taking Miss Pross in it had much engaged Mr. Lorry's attention. It was not merely desirable to avoid overloading the coach, but it was of the highest importance that the time occupied in examining it and its passengers, should be reduced to the utmost; since their escape might depend on the saving of only a few seconds here and there. Finally, he had proposed, after anxious consideration, that Miss Pross and Jerry, who were at liberty to leave the city, should leave it at three o'clock in the lightest-wheeled conveyance known to that period. Unencumbered with luggage, they would soon overtake the coach, and passing it, would order its horses in advance, and greatly facilitate its progress during the precious hours of the night, when delay was the most to be dreaded.

Seeing in this arrangement the hope of rendering real service in that pressing emergency, Miss Pross hailed it with joy. She and Jerry had beheld the coach start, had known who it was that Barsad brought, had passed some ten minutes in tortures of suspense, and were now concluding their arrangements to follow the coach, even as Madame Defarge, taking her way through the streets, now drew nearer and nearer to the else-deserted lodging in which they held their consultation.

'Now what do you think, Mr. Cruncher,' said Miss Pross, whose agitation was so great that she could hardly speak, 'what do you think of our not starting from this court-yard? Another carriage having already gone from here to-day, it might awaken suspicion.'

'My opinion, miss,' returned Mr. Cruncher, 'is as you're right.'

'I am so distracted with fear and hope for our precious creatures,' said Miss Pross, wildly crying, 'that I am incapable of forming any plan. Are *you* capable of forming any plan, my dear good Mr. Cruncher?'

Jerry Cruncher was not; but finally it was agreed that he should go to the posting-house, stop the vehicle and horses from coming to the court-yard, and take Miss Pross in near the cathedral door between the two towers.

'I am doubtful,' said Mr. Cruncher, hesitating and shaking

his head, 'about leaving of you. We don't know what may happen.'

'Heaven knows we don't,' returned Miss Pross, 'but have no fear for me. Take me in at the cathedral, at three o'clock, or as near it as you can, and I am sure it will be better than our going from here. I feel certain of it. There! Bless you, Mr. Cruncher! Think—not of me, but of the lives that may depend on both of us.'

This exordium, and Miss Pross's two hands in quite agonised entreaty clasping his, decided Mr. Cruncher. With an encouraging nod or two, he immediately went out to alter the arrangements, and left her by herself to follow as she had proposed.

Afraid, in her extreme perturbation, of the loneliness of the deserted rooms, Miss Pross got a basin of cold water and began laving her eyes, which were swollen and red, constantly pausing and looking round to see that there was no one watching her. In one of these pauses she recoiled and cried out, for she saw a figure standing in the room.

Madame Defarge looked coldly at her, and said, 'The wife of Evrémonde: where is she?'

It flashed upon Miss Pross's mind that the doors were all standing open, and would suggest the flight. Her first act was to shut them. There were four in the room, and she shut them all. She then placed herself before the door of the chamber which Lucie had occupied.

Madame Defarge's dark eyes followed her through this rapid movement, and rested on her when it was finished. She saw a tight, hard, wiry woman before her, as Mr. Lorry had seen in the same figure a woman with a strong hand, in the years gone by. She knew full well that Miss Pross was the family's devoted friend; Miss Pross knew full well that Madame Defarge was the family's malevolent enemy.

'On my way yonder,' said Madame Defarge, with a slight movement of her hand towards the fatal spot, 'where they reserve my chair and my knitting for me, I am come to make my compliments to her in passing. I wish to see her.'

'I know that your intentions are evil,' said Miss Pross, 'and you may depend upon it, I'll hold my own against them.'

Each spoke in her own language; neither understood the other's words; both were very watchful, and intent to deduce from look and manner, what the unintelligible words meant.

'It will do her no good to keep herself concealed from me at this moment,' said Madame Defarge. 'Good patriots will know what that means. Let me see her. Go tell her that I wish to see her. Do you hear? Either tell her that I demand to see her, or stand out of the way of the door and let me go to her!' This, with an angry explanatory wave of her right arm.

Neither of them for a single moment released the other's eyes. Madame Defarge had not moved from the spot where she stood when Miss Pross first became aware of her; but she now advanced one step.

'I am a Briton,' said Miss Pross; 'I am desperate. I don't care an English Twopence for myself. I know that the longer I keep you here, the greater hope there is for my Ladybird. I'll not leave a handful of that dark hair upon your head, if you lay a finger on me!'

But, her courage was of that emotional nature that it brought the irrepressible tears into her eyes. This was a courage that Madame Defarge so little comprehended as to mistake for weakness. 'Ha, ha!' she laughed, 'you poor wretch! What are you worth!' Then she raised her voice and called out, 'Citizen Doctor! Wife of Evrémonde! Child of Evrémonde! Any person but this miserable fool, answer the Citizeness Defarge!'

Perhaps the following silence, perhaps some latent disclosure in the expression of Miss Pross's face, whispered to Madame Defarge that they were gone. Three of the doors she opened swiftly, and looked in.

'Those rooms are all in disorder, there has been hurried packing, there are odds and ends upon the ground. There is no one in that room behind you! Let me look.'

'Never!' said Miss Pross, who understood the request as perfectly as Madame Defarge understood the answer.

'If they are not in that room, they are gone, and can be pursued and brought back,' said Madame Defarge to herself.

'As long as you don't know whether they are in that room or not, you are uncertain what to do,' said Miss Pross to *her*-self; 'and you shall not know that, if I can prevent your knowing it; and know that, or not know that, you shall not leave here while I can hold you.'

'I have been in the streets from the first, nothing has stopped me, I will tear you to pieces, but I will have you from that door,' said Madame Defarge.

Madame Defarge made at the door. Miss Pross, on the instinct of the moment, seized her round the waist in both her arms, and held her tight. It was in vain for Madame Defarge to struggle and to strike; Miss Pross, with the vigorous tenacity of love, always so much stronger than hate, clasped her tight, and even lifted her from the floor in the struggle that they had. The two hands of Madame Defarge buffeted and tore her face; but, Miss Pross, with her head down, held her round the waist, and clung to her with more than the hold of a drowning woman.

Soon, Madame Defarge's hands ceased to strike, and felt at her encircled waist. 'It is under my arm,' said Miss Pross, in smothered tones, 'you shall not draw it. I am stronger than you, I bless Heaven for it. I'll hold you till one or other of us faints or dies!'

Madame Defarge's hands were at her bosom. Miss Pross looked up, saw what it was, struck at it, struck out a flash and a crash, and stood alone—blinded with smoke.

All this was in a second. As the smoke cleared, leaving an awful stillness, it passed out on the air, like the soul of the furious woman whose body lay lifeless on the ground.

In the first fright and horror of her situation, Miss Pross passed the body as far from it as she could, and ran down the stairs to call for fruitless help. Happily, she bethought herself of the consequences of what she did, in time to check herself and go back. It was dreadful to go in at the door again; but, she did go in, to get the bonnet and other things that she must wear. These she put on, out on the staircase, first shutting and locking the door and taking away the key. She then sat down on the stairs a few moments to breathe and to cry, and then got up and hurried away.

By good fortune she had a veil on her bonnet, or she could hardly have gone along the streets without being stopped. By good fortune, too, she was naturally so peculiar in appearance as not to show disfigurement like any other woman. She needed both advantages, for the marks of griping fingers were deep in her face, and her hair was torn, and her dress (hastily composed with unsteady hands) was clutched and dragged a hundred ways.

In crossing the bridge, she dropped the door key in the

river. Arriving at the cathedral some few minutes before her escort, and waiting there, she thought, what if the key were already taken in a net, what if it were identified, what if the door were opened.—In the midst of these fluttering thoughts, Jerry Cruncher appeared, took her in, and took her away.

'Is there any noise in the streets?' she asked him.

'The usual noises,' Mr. Cruncher replied; and looked surprised by the question and by her aspect.

'I don't hear you,' said Miss Pross. 'What do you say?'

It was in vain for Mr. Cruncher to repeat what he said: Miss Pross could not hear him. 'So I'll nod my head,' thought Mr. Cruncher, amazed, 'at all events she'll see that.' And she did.

'Is there any noise in the streets now?' asked Miss Pross again, presently.

Again Mr. Cruncher nodded his head.

'I don't hear it.'

'Gone deaf in a hour?' said Mr. Cruncher, ruminating, with his mind much disturbed; 'wot's come to her?'

'I feel,' said Miss Pross, 'as if there had been a flash and a crash, and that crash was the last thing I should ever hear in this life.'

'Blest if she ain't in a queer condition!' said Mr. Cruncher, more and more disturbed. 'Wot can she have been a takin', to keep her courage up? Hark! There's the roll of them dreadful carts! You can hear that, miss?'

'I can hear,' said Miss Pross, seeing that he spoke to her, 'nothing. O, my good man, there was first a great crash, and then a great stillness, and that stillness seems to be fixed and unchangeable, never to be broken any more as long as my life lasts.'

'If she don't hear the roll of those dreadful carts, now very nigh their journey's end,' said Mr. Cruncher, glancing over his shoulder, 'it's my opinion that indeed she never will hear anything else in this world.'

And indeed she never did.

Along the Paris streets, the death-carts rumble, hollow and harsh. Six tumbrils roll along the streets. As the sombre wheels go round, they seem to plough up a long crooked furrow among the populace in the streets. Ridges of faces are thrown to this side and to that, and the ploughs go steadily onward. So used are the regular inhabitants of the houses to the spectacle, that in many windows there are no people, and in some the occupation of the hands is not so much as suspended, while the eyes survey the faces in the tumbrils. Here and there, the inmate has visitors to see the sight; then he points his finger, with something of the complacency of a curator or authorized exponent, to this cart and to this, and seems to tell who sat here yesterday, and who there the day before.

There is a guard of sundry horsemen riding abreast of the tumbrils, and faces are often turned up to some of them, and they are asked some question. It would seem to be always the same question, for, it is always followed by a press of people towards the third cart. The horsemen abreast of that cart, frequently point out one man in it with their swords. The leading curiosity is, to know which is he; he stands at the back of the tumbril with his head bent down, to converse with a mere girl who sits on the side of the cart, and holds his hand. He has no curiosity or care for the scene about him, and always speaks to the girl. Here and there in the long street of St. Honoré, cries are raised against him. If they move him at all, it is only to a quiet smile, as he shakes his hair a little more loosely about his face.

On the steps of a church, awaiting the coming-up of the tumbrils, stands the Spy and prison-sheep. He looks into the first of them: not there. He looks into the second: not there. He already asks himself, 'Has he sacrificed me?' when his face clears, as he looks into the third.

'Which is Evrémonde?' says a man behind him.

'That. At the back there.'

'With his hand in the girl's?'

'Yes.'

The man cries, 'Down, Evrémonde! To the Guillotine all aristocrats! Down, Evrémonde!'

'Hush, hush!' the Spy entreats him, timidly.

'And why not, citizen?'

'He is going to pay the forfeit: it will be paid in five minutes more. Let him be at peace.'

But the man continuing to exclaim, 'Down, Evrémonde!' the face of Evrémonde is for a moment turned towards him. Evrémonde then sees the Spy, and looks attentively at him, and goes his way.

The clocks are on the stroke of three, and the furrow ploughed among the populace is turning round, to come on into the place of execution, and end. The ridges thrown to this side and to that, now crumble in and close behind the last plough as it passes on, for all are following to the Guillotine. In front of it, seated in chairs, as in a garden of public diversion, are a number of women, busily knitting. On one of the foremost chairs, stands The Vengeance, looking about for her friend.

'Thérèse!' she cries, in her shrill tones. 'Who has seen her? Thérèse Defarge!'

'She never missed before,' says a knitting-woman of the sisterhood.

'No; nor will she miss now,' cries The Vengeance, petulantly. 'Thérèse!'

'Louder,' the woman recommends.

Ay! Louder, Vengeance, much louder, and still she will scarcely hear thee. Louder yet, Vengeance, with a little oath or so added, and yet it will hardly bring her.

'Bad Fortune!' cries The Vengeance, stamping her foot in the chair, 'and here are the tumbrils! And Evrémonde will be despatched in a wink, and she not here! See her knitting in my hand, and her empty chair ready for her. I cry with vexation and disappointment!'

As The Vengeance descends from her elevation to do it, the tumbrils begin to discharge their loads. The ministers of Sainte Guillotine are robed and ready. Crash!—A head is held up, and the knitting-women who scarcely lifted their eyes to look at it a moment ago when it could think and speak, count One.

The second tumbril empties and moves on; the third comes up. Crash!—And the knitting-women, never faltering or pausing in their work, count Two.

The supposed Evrémonde descends, and the seamstress is lifted out next after him. He has not relinquished her patient hand in getting out, but still holds it as he promised. He gently places her with her back to the crashing engine that constantly whirrs up and falls, and she looks into his face and thanks him.

'But for you, dear stranger, I should not be so composed, for I am naturally a poor little thing, faint of heart; nor should I have been able to raise my thoughts to Him who was put to death, that we might have hope and comfort here to-day. I think you were sent to me by Heaven.'

'Or you to me,' says Sydney Carton. 'Keep your eyes upon me, dear child, and mind no other object.'

'I mind nothing while I hold your hand. I shall mind nothing when I let it go, if they are rapid.'

'They will be rapid. Fear not!'

The two stand in the fast-thinning throng of victims, but they speak as if they were alone. Eye to eye, voice to voice, hand to hand, heart to heart, these two children of the Universal Mother, else so wide apart and differing, have come together on the dark highway, to repair home together, and to rest in her bosom.

'You comfort me so much! Am I to kiss you now? Is the moment come?'

'Yes.'

She kisses his lips; he kisses hers; they solemnly bless each other. The spare hand does not tremble as he releases it; nothing worse than a sweet, bright constancy is in the patient face. She goes next before him—is gone; the knitting-women count Twenty-Two.

'I am the Resurrection and the Life, saith the Lord: he that believeth in me, though he were dead, yet shall he live: and whosoever liveth and believeth in me shall never die.'

The murmuring of many voices, the upturning of many faces, the pressing on of many footsteps in the outskirts of the crowd, so that it swells forward in a mass, like one great heave of water, all flashes away. Twenty-three.

They said of him, about the city that night, that it was the peacefullest man's face ever beheld there.

One of the most remarkable sufferers by the same axe—a woman—had asked at the foot of the same scaffold, not long before, to be allowed to write down the thoughts that were inspiring her. If he had given an utterance to his, and they were prophetic, they would have been these:

'I see Barsad, Defarge, The Vengeance, the Jurymen, the Judges, long ranks of the new oppressors who have risen on the destruction of the old, perishing by this retributive instrument, before it shall cease out of its present use. I see a beautiful city and a brilliant people rising from this abyss, and, in their struggles to be truly free, in their triumphs and defeats, through long long years to come, I see the evil of this time and of the previous time of which this is the natural birth, gradually making expiation for itself and wearing out.

'I see the lives for which I lay down my life, peaceful, useful, prosperous and happy, in that England which I shall see no more. I see Her with a child upon her bosom, who bears my name. I see her father, aged and bent, but otherwise restored, and faithful to all men in his healing office, and at peace. I see the good old man, so long their friend, in ten years' time enriching them with all he has, and passing tranquilly to his reward.

'I see that I hold a sanctuary in their hearts, and in the hearts of their descendants, generations hence. I see that child who lay upon her bosom and who bore my name, a man winning his way up in that path of life which once was mine. I see him, foremost of just judges and honoured men, bringing a boy of my name, with a forehead that I know and golden hair, to this place—then fair to look upon, with not a trace of this day's disfigurement—and I hear him tell the child my story, with a tender and a faltering voice.

'It is a far, far better thing that I do, than I have ever done; it is a far, far better rest that I go to than I have ever known.'